LIZARD WELLS

After losing his whole family to a bloodthirsty army patrol, Ben Brooke takes to the desolate Ozark snowline. Years later, he returns to the town called Lizard Wells, where the guilty soldiers have degenerated into guerrillas, bringing brutal disorder to the town. Also living there is the tough Erma Flagg — and more importantly, Moses, a young Cheyenne half-breed . . . After a wild thunderstorm crushes the town, Ben, in desperate need of help, chooses to step single-handedly into a final reckoning.

X

CALEB RAND

LIZARD WELLS

Complete and Unabridged

LINFORD
Leicester

First published in Great Britain in 2007 by
Robert Hale Limited
London

First Linford Edition
published 2008
by arrangement with
Robert Hale Limited
London

British Library CIP Data

Rand, Caleb
  Lizard Wells.—Large print ed.—
  Linford western library
  1. Western stories
  2. Large type books
  I. Title
  823.9'2 [F]

  ISBN 978–1–84782–358–8

Published by
F. A. Thorpe (Publishing)
Anstey, Leicestershire

Set by Words & Graphics Ltd.
Anstey, Leicestershire
Printed and bound in Great Britain by
T. J. International Ltd., Padstow, Cornwall

This book is printed on acid-free paper

For RMB & DCB & WCB

1

Early in 1860, the Dog Leg Stage was established between Jefferson City and Sedalia. It was officially for mail, but mainly it carried a rag-bag of frontiersmen, most of them headstrong and well armed.

As new veins of gold and silver were discovered in the Ozarks, the east-west advance increased, and white renegades, as well as the Kiowa and Cheyenne made their own gain. The stagecoaches were frequently captured and burned, any occupants robbed and killed, the horses seized. For the tribes protecting their own lands and way of life, it meant blankets, tools and a bounty of firearms — occasionally the abduction of children. Drivers were reluctant to make the cross-country journeys and were hard to come by.

In the town of Lizard Wells, a miner

and two land speculators destined for Sedalia had waited two days for the through stage. But a rider had brought in news of Indian trouble, and they were prepared to wait another day before going on. They voiced their fears to the driver, and suggested they all go with the next stage as a combined team. It was a primitive instinct of safety in numbers, a more effective defence against attack.

'That's yer choice, gents, but I'm paid to take this coach on at noon, an' that's what I'm aimin' to do,' the driver responded confidently.

There were no ready takers for the ride, and the coach was filled with dry goods and army provision boxes. There was one, however, who decided to make the journey. She was a determined woman, and the driver said she'd have to make her own space. She was an amiable, but tough frontier entrepreneur. Her name was Erma Flagg, and she was travelling north on a personal matter.

They were rough, turbulent times, and the driver considered it an obligation to mention that Rumer Wheat treat the lady with respect. Wheat was the sutler who was carrying the profitable goods for the soldiers of Fort Denton. One of the men who wasn't going, called for Erma to rethink her journey.

'It ain't no square dance you're headed for, lady,' he warned.

'No, you're right there,' she said, 'but if the driver reckons he can make it, I'll take my chances.'

'She's got more balls than you three put together,' the sutler shouted at the backs of the departing men. 'No offence, ma'am,' he added. 'That's the best o' compliments.'

They climbed aboard the coach. The sutler rode alongside the driver as reluctant shotgun, and Erma wedged herself among his pile of trade.

The driver gathered up the reins and looked around him. 'Anyway, who'd want to stay in this Godforsaken hole,' he quipped, then called out the moving-off ritual to his team of horses.

Except for the overnight stopover, there were no comfortable halts along the route, just coldharbour relays. Between these stations the coach rolled along at good speed, the changes usually made in less than ten minutes.

There were two scheduled stops before they reached Sand Flats. It was from where the rider had brought bad news. In breathtaking style, he'd told of war-painted savages and their fearful aggression.

At each stop the sutler got more anxious, less keen on his profit from the army. But the driver remained confident. 'This stage is goin' to be real mindful o' time,' he told them.

'You should be real mindful o' protectin' this here lady,' Wheat carped, as he climbed back onto the riding board.

'I'm thinkin' it was her own idea, an' she don't appear to be sick in the head or nothin'. I'd put money on her to give as good as she gets. In fact, if we meet any o' them redskins, I'll invite her out for a powwow.' The driver winked down at Erma as he flicked the reins.

For two further hours, the stage rollicked across the flats. The horses were enjoying the pull as they approached a shallow creek that wasn't far from the trouble spot of a week before.

'Look to your guns, sutler,' the driver warned. 'If anythin' happens, don't go jawbone on me. Start shootin'.'

Erma craned her neck out of the coach window. 'How 'bout me, driver?'

The driver looked at Wheat. 'Bless her heart. She reminds me o' me. Pick 'em up, girls,' he then shouted. The horses shied, then bucked in their stride. Off the trail, they'd seen a coyote pack. The ferocious dogs snapped and snarled as they dragged at bones and bloody meat. It was where one of the horses from the attacked stage had met its end.

'That's where they took 'em,' the driver remarked, as they jounced through at speed. He looked around him uneasily.

'You reckon we're on our own, out here?' Wheat asked.

'Depends whether it's sidewinder or Injun,' the driver said thoughtfully. 'You ain't *ever* on your own.'

Snake Pass was a few miles further north of the flats. It was on the second part of the dog-leg, and the trail ran between low rock formations that wound along the side of the creek.

It was early evening as the coach slowed in its approach to the pass. Heat was still rising from the ground and, in the shimmer, mounted riders were visible from a quarter-mile out.

Wheat spoke nervously to the driver. 'There, ahead.'

The driver never flinched, or took his eyes off the trail ahead. 'I seen 'em. Hold tight,' he warned, sending the team into a full gallop.

★   ★   ★

6

From his war-painted pony, Long Moon gripped his lance. It was decorated with eagle feathers, and carried blue and yellow beads which he ran against his thumb. He raised his left hand to shield his eyes, and watched the stagecoach as it lurched in to a sudden clip for the pass. He shook his head, turned to Brown Bear and spoke slowly. 'He's whipping the horses. They're going to race through.' He pointed into the low, undulating rocks. 'Use the ground . . . the mesquite as cover. Shoot the lead horse.'

Brown Bear looked critical, but his chief responded quickly. 'Keep the young ones quiet. Move now.'

As Brown Bear swung away, Long Moon held in his pony, squinted as the Dog Leg Stagecoach advanced. It was close enough now for the old Indian to see the faces of the two who rode on top. He recognized the man who sat next to the driver as one who supplied the bluecoats with whiskey and tobacco. Long Moon thought of his small tribe, their fight to retain their camps and hunting grounds. He'd tried to avoid the whites, the men with horses, mules and wagons that blighted their land. But they came on fast, in increasing numbers to plunder and kill.

He heard a short animal yip. It meant that Brown Bear was well hidden and positioned with his rifle. The Indian chief looked around him, satisfied. Apart from a lizard that skittered from its hiding place, he couldn't see any unnatural sign, and he stepped his pony a pace forward. He lifted his right arm, looked towards the Ozark timberline and Creek Lakes, then shook the point of his lance three times towards the east. A low guttural noise came from his throat, then he was gone, his war paint and deer skins fusing with the shapes and textures that edged the pass.

2

The stagecoach creaked and rattled wildly in its headlong dash. The horses were fresh and strong, and they thrust their glistening heads forward. The driver was calling for more effort, cracking his whip when one of the lead pair suddenly slewed, then buckled into a dive against its partner. It was fractionally after the unmistakable crack of a rifle shot from up ahead.

Wheat and Erma were ready and fired simultaneously from the coach, but it was into thin air. As they took the first twist in the pass, the riders had withdrawn into the low, layered rocks.

The dying animal had brought the coach to a halt, and the driver was staring wildly about him. He sprang from the box, and ran to cut free the harness. The horse had taken a fatal bullet, and its hind legs jerked, and its neck arched in its last few seconds of life.

It was then, with terrifying cries, that the Cheyenne braves appeared from cover. They were brandishing feathered lances, and firing rifles, but they held off from the stage because Wheat and Erma were again measuring out a barrage of gunfire. Huddled behind the dead horse, the driver yelled curses at the Indians and grabbed for his pistol. He flung himself low across the horse's back and emptied his cylinder into the shrieking mob.

Wheat and Erma continued their fire and brought down two of the young, painted braves. The Indians' unrelenting clamour broke into shrill, excited yelps, and they whirled their ponies, before once again disappearing into the bleak landscape.

'Now cut him loose,' shouted Wheat, grabbing up the reins again. But the driver didn't move. He lay still and silent across the broad belly of the dead horse.

The remaining horses were stamping the ground in alarm. Erma climbed from the coach, and Wheat handed down the reins. He leaped to the ground and ran with his head down. The driver had been hit twice and was already dead.

Erma walked up, her breath coming in short, heavy spasms.

Wheat got to his feet and had a long look at the distant mountains. 'He was a bold driver, Erma, but it's been the death of him. Some day the Indians are goin' to pay for all this.' He grasped the driver by his leather jerkin, pulled him into the coach, and laid him across his supply boxes.

Erma cut loose the dead horse. She tied its lead partner on behind, and flung the front harness around the next pair. Wheat was sitting ready to move off, and he looked sharply at Erma as she climbed up beside him. 'You want to go on?'

Erma was holding the shotgun, and she looked straight ahead. 'My ol' ma would've said not to meet trouble halfway. Right now she's laid up real poorly in Sedalia. So, yeah, I'm goin' on.'

Wheat blew air through his teeth and looked across the heads of the straining horses. 'But not just yet,' he told her.

The coach had been surrounded by a band of about twenty of the Cheyenne. They'd changed their tactics, sat their ponies arrogant and silent.

'Goddammit,' Erma yelled. Without thinking, she swung up the shotgun, leapt to her feet and fired both barrels out at the mounted braves. Wheat cursed and made a grab for his big revolver. The Indians were momentarily stunned by the explosive retaliation, and those nearest the coach were being bucked by their ponies in fear and confusion.

Erma's hat had flown from her head. The Indians saw her flowing fair hair as it tumbled around her shoulders, and their reaction was immediate. There was no doubt in Rumer Wheat's mind that the Cheyenne were thinking the same as him. Erma's cavalry breeches only added to the illusion.

'Get inside,' Wheat yelled, and they both rolled off their seats, throwing their legs and bodies into opposite sides of the coach. They knew they weren't going anywhere then and in fear and defiance they piled more fire out of the windows. 'Get the boxes around you,' he said, shoving the driver down to the floor of the coach. They lay in silence for nearly five minutes before the sutler decided to have a look out. He squeezed himself across to the other side of the coach. There was nothing to be seen, except the settling dust from the Indians' ponies. 'They've gone, Erma, an' they won't be back.'

Erma eased herself into a corner of the stage, her feet avoiding the body of the driver. 'How'd you know that? I'm sittin' tight. Do you know what they'd do to *me*?'

'Ah, but that's just it. They don't know it's *you*, Erma. They think you're

Custer . . . the long hair. He's a long ways from here, but believe me, they got a real dreadful fear between their legs.'

Erma laughed nervously. 'Custer, eh? Well, I did hear tell he's a pretty lookin' feller. But I can't think what General George'd be doin' out here sittin' on candy.'

'We'll lie up here an' wait for the next coach to pass.' Wheat looked nervously at Erma and noticed a trickle of blood from the sleeve of her jacket. 'You been hit.'

'Nothin' more'n a mozzie sting. Your beads an' blankets got more damage done to 'em.'

It was nearly full dark when they heard the coach approaching. It was from Sedalia, and heading towards them. As he brought his team through the pass, the driver swerved and pulled up alongside. Wheat took most of the credit for saving his own provisions and, in the grim circumstances, suggested that Erma travel back to the relative safety of Lizard Wells.

The man who rode shotgun with the incoming coach, foolishly agreed to transfer. Wheat's eagerness for profit had won out, and together they'd take his supplies on a few miles to the night stop and trade store. From atop the returning coach, Erma looked down as the sutler walked up.

Wheat placed a hand on the kicking board and sighed. 'I have to go on, you understand, but I hope to have the pleasure, ma'am, of meetin' you again. Perhaps bein' of service. An' when you get to see your ma, you can tell her from me, she ain't done too bad by her daughter.'

Erma smiled weakly. 'Why, I'll live on, just wonderin' what service you could be meanin', Mr Wheat,' she answered without sincerity.

A small reputation for survival had been made, and for a short while, Erma Flagg became the stuff of local legend.

3

It was the end of an era for the trappers — the mountain men. The demand for beaver skin had declined in favour of seal fur and silk. But there was still plenty of game in the mountains, and Ben Brooke decided he could live well enough by hunting.

Through many seasons he enjoyed the life of hunting deer and rabbit, the staples of the Cheyenne. He kept his own counsel, went alone, and only killed when meat was needed. He had tentative, minor skirmishes with the Indians, but generally they kept their distance and he travelled unharmed. He took his time in building a cabin along the headwaters of the River Piney, in the deep timberline of the Ozarks. He felt himself grow with the richness and culture of the land, living out the happiest moments of his life. As the years had passed, he'd become trusted by the small bands of Indians and began to make trade.

After five years, he'd earned the respect and acceptance of the people whose land he shared. Except for his colour and a splendid moustache, Ben Brooke, dressed in buckskins and moccasins, took to the spirit and appearance of a Cheyenne.

★   ★   ★

It was during early summer — the Moon of Flowers — that Ben had his first meeting with Blue Sky.

He was standing with a few Cheyenne on the banks of the Piney. They were watching the first canoes arrive. He'd never seen such dugouts. They were slim and black, long and smooth like the body of an eel.

Chief Long Moon moved close to Ben. 'The start of the hunting season. Pawnee and the far travelling Seneca are bringing gifts,' he explained briefly.

For a long time, Ben had been trading marten and beaver. It was in return for silver, that the Cheyenne band scraped from a high mountain lode.

Elders of the tribe wore blankets embroidered with yellow and brilliant turquoise. Long Moon was wrapped in grey-wolf skin. He was pleased with Ben's presence, and he spoke with quiet satisfaction. 'We have done well with our trade, Ben.'

'That we have, Long Moon. That we have.'

'We have lived at peace around our own fires.'

Ben nodded. After nearly five years, he was also pleased at his affinity with the tribe.

Long Moon gave Ben a penetrating look, his wrinkles creasing deep across his forehead. 'Now we shall eat together . . . share the same feast for the hunting.'

Ben was invited to sit close to Long Moon, who told him tales of his battles with the white man, and the spread of bones across the land of lakes and mountains. 'You look like them, Ben. It's your heart that's different, and that's good.'

Ben gave the chief a wry look. 'Good for who, Long Moon?' he asked.

'Hah, that's *you*, my friend. Otherwise a young Cheyenne brave would have it roasting on the end of a skinning knife.' Long Moon clasped his knees. He chuckled softly, indicated the food displayed around them.

There were berry cakes, baked tiger lily bulbs and fern root. For the first time Ben tasted the Pawnee gifts of clam and mountain salmon.

He was eating a roast squirrel, rubbing juices from his hands and face with moss when he looked up to see Blue Sky, laughing and mocking his appearance. She was wearing a cedar-bark skirt for the potlatch, and there was red paint on her face and in the parting of her hair. She called him 'No Knife', and then quickly disappeared among the trees. Ben heard a soft echo of his bestowed name, and he sat comfortable, watching the embers from the cooking fires crack and glitter into the forest night.

* * *

During the long summer months, Ben enjoyed many visits and feasts with the tribe. Long Moon introduced him to family customs and explained legend and myth of the Cheyenne. Ben's relationship with Blue Sky became close, and it was obvious from women elders of the tribe that his attentions were acceptable and looked upon with amusement and favour.

In the same year, and before full winter set in, Blue Sky had taken him close to the burial place of her father Josef Fish. It was an eerie and silent place, edging a cholla stand by the waters of a shallow river that fed Horse Creek Lakes. The scant remains of her father were lying on a platform of logs, almost indistinguishable from the thin, gnarled branches that provided support, head high from the ground. Tatters of a blanket that had once wrapped the body, shredded down from the raw, crumbling platform. Blue Sky touched the bleached remnants of a tribal garment that hung unmoved and poignant in the chilly breeze.

Ben watched an imperious crow cautiously strut the sacred platform, although the raptors and buzzards had finished their grizzly work a long time past. Under the tree lay the time-whitened bones of a sacrificed pony, and Ben felt respect and intrigue, as Blue Sky kneeled to remove a fragment from the thinly scattered pile.

There was so much he wanted to ask about superstitions, medicine and spiritual meanings, but he was embarrassed and still unsure because he was a white man, an outsider in a close, family world.

The piece of bone would be scraped and fashioned into a small gift from

Blue Sky. She would make it into a knife handle, would slip it into his hand just before the wedding ceremony when she became his wife.

4

A hubbub of voices rose from the wide-clearing around Fort Denton. More than a hundred people, mostly whites, but some Indian traders and half-breeds with their sled dogs and camp gear had already arrived. More were trailing in from the wilderness — wolfers, trappers, mountain men. They were here to celebrate New Year's Day. Some had even brought families, and the fort had been designated to play host.

A half-dozen deer and pig carcasses were already roasting above red-hot charcoal pits. Fur trading would wait until after the feast, but gossip and the trading of news was loud and lively. Inside the fort, fiddlers were trying out new and old tunes, for the dancing would last through the night.

Only in the group of men near the

cages of the fighting dogs was the festive mood wanting. These were the men who'd looked forward for months to the cruel sport of the fighting pits and the betting. But now they were staring hard at a notice that had been nailed to a post. 'Dog Fights are Forbidden', it stated above the official order and stamp of the Army Administrator.

Toward this group strode Bolton McKay, the boorish army scout. Behind him, in its sled-mounted cage was a heavily muscled, Old Country Bulldog.

'What the hell's goin' on here?' the big man queried. 'Why ain't the fights started?'

Most of the thwarted men turned to face him. 'There'll be no more fightin',' one of the men answered. 'There's a new regulation. You can read it for yourself.'

McKay stared back at him. Then he cursed. 'I don't know what part o' you's the old lady, Wheat, but no one's tellin' me I can't fight my dog with any other

24

cur, if I've a mind. We'll set 'em up right now, goddammit. If any big city, wig an' pen man interferes, he can meet me in the pit when we've finished.'

Disgruntlement lifted from the faces of the dog owners. In anticipation, they gathered around McKay and the snarling black-eyed beast in his cage.

After a moment's thought, Rumer Wheat laughed. 'Yeah, you're right,' he agreed. 'I'll even wager a bottle o' double rectified, an' a dozen beaver pelts that my Snapper takes your devil.'

'Twenty, says my dog bites his ass off,' McKay countered.

'You got twenty pelts?' Wheat showed his chawstained teeth as he challenged McKay.

McKay reached out and clutched the sutler's coat front with a huge, dirty fist. 'Makes no difference. I'm takin' *your* fur,' he snarled aggressively.

Willing hands moved the cages of the bulldog and Snapper into the openings at either side of the log-walled fighting pit.

Around the pit's rim, the crowd shoved in to watch. Betting was already in progress when the ends of the two cages were pulled up for the dogs to come out.

Suspicious of an unexpected cruelty, the bulldog was slow to move into the small arena. He hardly looked at the other dog, and the hoots of the surrounding mob seemed to bewilder him. For a moment, McKay fumed silently. He was thinking the dog had lost his fighting spirit.

Wheat's dog was a malamute of two seasons' fighting experience. He moved at a half-crouch, circling the pit. He was shorter and stockier than the bulldog, though he weighed as much. Without warning he sprang.

For a second or two it seemed that the Malamute had got his death grip, but in a flash the picture changed. Breaking free, the bulldog counter-attacked, used its muscle with shocking ferocity. The crowd yelled, and in the uproar, more bets were changed.

Next, the scream of a dog in anguish and pain breached the tumult. In the pit, a blood-streaked bulldog stood menacingly over the weakly moving body of Snapper.

McKay's heavy laugh broke the silence. 'I'm warnin' you, Wheat, if you want that animal to live, get him out o' there.'

'Call that killer o' yours off first,' Wheat yelled back.

McKay slapped the side of the pit and bulldog whirled, leaped at the teasing hand. A moment later, Wheat had vaulted into pit and in one rushed move he heaved his injured dog up and over the rim. Barely in time, strong hands dragged at Wheat as the bull-dog's teeth clicked inches from his heels.

McKay tossed the pile of furs he'd won onto his fighter's cage and grinned at the waiting crowd. 'Hardly enough here for a new coat. So who's next?' he asked.

'There ain't one,' a new voice levelled out.

The crush eased off as Ben Brooke elbowed his way to the side of the pit.

'Let the dogs be,' he followed up. 'What pack's the bulldog with?'

McKay moved forward, threat in the swing of his thick shoulders. 'Mine. What the hell's it to you, mister?' he challenged.

'He's hurt too,' Ben replied. 'Get him out o' there, an' get him taken care of.'

McKay drew himself up to the younger man, and a leer spread across his raw-featured face. 'How about, I let the dog take care o' *you*?' he shouted for all to hear.

With his foot pressed down on Ben's toe, McKay suddenly swung an elbow and shoved hard. The top rail of the log wall caught Ben's legs and he stumbled backwards, toppled awkwardly into the pit.

'Hah. Now let's see you use that long nose to pry yourself out o' there,' McKay sneered.

A snarl, warbled gruffly in the bulldog's throat. With his own hot blood and Snapper's staining the hard-packed ground, he saw Ben's shape as a new enemy. He crouched, began a slow, circling of the fallen man.

Raising the pitch of the snarl from the bulldog, Ben turned on his shoulder, pressed his hands into the hard-packed dirt. 'Stay back,' he said quietly but firmly. 'This really ain't work for any aspirin' young feller.' As he spoke, he rose slowly to his feet. He turned his face towards the bulldog, but avoided the threat of direct eye contact.

The dog's harsh snarling changed to a low growl.

'Yeah, that's better,' Ben's voice soothed on. 'Let me take you away from all this, boy. I know o' good places where you don't get bit back.'

The dog's hackles lowered a bit and his tail switched. A throaty whine came from him as he stretched to sniff Ben's upturned hand.

'If this sort o' thing came natural, by now you'd have chewed my arm off at the elbow,' Ben continued, as he rubbed his fingertips into the soft tissue around the dog's jawline.

'Haw haw, look at your cur now, McKay,' Rumer Wheat sneered. 'It's more like a killer kitten.' At first the crowd chuckled doubtfully, then they laughed with glee.

McKay cursed under his breath as he picked up a leash rope. He swung the noose over the bulldog's head and tightened, dragged it struggling towards the cage.

Ben stood up. 'You ain't up to keepin' any critter that's smarter than you, mister,' he said. 'So I'll take him, an' fight you *now* if I have to.'

McKay sniffed unpleasantly and tied the dog's rope to the cage. 'You don't *have* to, but I'd *like* it,' he shouted hoarsely, swinging into the arena. He held out his hand as if to shake on the issue, simultaneously lashed out with a free-fighting-style kick.

The edge of McKay's boot caught Ben unawares, rasped his jaw with enough force to knock him down. He rolled to escape a second kick, came back lightly to his toes. He dodged McKay's wild pile-driver of a punch and cranked upwards with his fist. With the full weight of Ben's powerful surge behind it, the blow took the breath from McKay as it slammed deep into his belly. With a brutal doggedness learned from the Cheyenne, Ben chopped in more wounding blows. He hammered the neck and upper ribs, then lower to the big scout's sides and kidneys.

The mob bayed and, fighting its rope, the bulldog growled its support.

Though he was far from losing consciousness, McKay stumbled and went down. He knew he was beaten, but fear and animal cunning took the place of rage. He struggled to his knees, then with a loud grunt, appeared to collapse.

'Let's get,' Ben called to the bulldog as he turned away. 'There ain't nothin' to keep us.'

Then, McKay coiled from the ground.

31

He lashed out a foot, and caught Ben low in the back. Ben gasped, staggered forward a pace and went down. Almost immediately, McKay had found his feet and flung himself forward onto him. The scout's coat curled open and he drew a broad-bladed knife from under his rancid skin shirt.

'I'll peel somethin' off you, mister,' he hissed. 'Turn you into a real goddamn red man.'

Rumer Wheat's fingers worked to untie the knot that was tethering the bulldog. 'Take your choice, boy,' he muttered. 'This is devil's work if ever I seen it.'

McKay had time only to glimpse the dog's hurtling shape, to raise his hands chest high before he was struck. Bowled over, the big man's body shuddered and rolled, his knees drawn in to his bearded chin. Then the bulldog's jaws locked onto his collar, snatching and tearing with convulsive movements.

Within seconds the pit was full of men. They pulled the snarling dog off

McKay, and someone thrust a wadded scarf between its jaws. Then they half lifted, half dragged him, into the cage and slammed the door back down.

Those nearest to McKay stared down at the man's painful, anger-filled features.

'Was his very own beast that tried to kill him. Get me a gun,' Wheat yelled eagerly.

One of the trappers tossed him an old single-action Colt, and he turned on the bulldog's cage. But, still shocked by the blow that McKay had landed in his back, Ben staggered forward.

'The man had the knife in his hand before the dog was loose,' he rasped. 'He was goin' to stick *me* with it. So, shoot this dog, an' I'll see you never ride another cat wagon.'

Thinking there'd be more fighting, the crowd howled with glee.

'I saw what happened. The scout full earned what he got,' an old mountain man said in a curious mixed tongue. From that moment, the crowd knew the conflicts were over, and dissatisfied, they stomped off in the direction of the roasting meats.

The mountain man lifted the door of the bulldog's cage. 'It's a wicked man that turns a dog the same way,' he rumbled through a beard-encrusted face. He smiled thoughtfully, spat a thin stream of dark juice. 'But you gone an' made a powerful bad enemy in Bolton Mckay. I suggest you leave an' take the mutt with you. Neither o' you are for settlin' in this neck o' the woods.'

Ben nodded his acceptance of the old man's advice. He'd have it no other way.

5

It was the tail end of August, and Captain Gideon Pelt was getting anxious. He'd left the fort with high expectations that the campaign would soon be over. He listened carefully to McKay, who'd reported that small bands of Cheyenne, Sioux and Pawnee were moving south, back from their tribal hunting grounds.

'Gimme a few more days, Cap'n,' the scout told Pelt. 'I can almost smell 'em.'

Less than a mile below the timberline of the Ozarks, Pelt sat frustrated and impatient in his tent. 'I'd be surprised if you could smell anythin' through that haze o' yours, McKay. You got one week.'

After McKay had left, Pelt took his telescope and stood in the fresh air for a while. He searched vainly across the high pine stands for anything that might give a lead to the whereabouts of an Indian trail or encampment.

On the third day, McKay reported back. He'd backtracked a small group of Cheyenne to a camp along the Piney. They were seventy-five miles out of Fort Denton, and Captain Pelt immediately swung his entire company towards the river. It was meant to be a campaign of repression and containment, but he made a decision to attack the following dawn.

Because of the pitch blackness, and closeness of the tree stands along the banks of the Piney, McKay had difficulty in locating the trail. It wasn't dawn as planned, but mid-morning before the troopers moved forward.

For the charge, Pelt had divided his company into two columns. The first, under Lieutenant Ketchum, attacked the band head on from the north, with orders to fire at will. The second column would inexplicably draw sabres and cross the river, then ride on through the small remuda.

The Indians were few in number, and travelling behind the hunting braves. They were mostly old men and women with their half-naked children. They could only flee in terror, under the sweeping blades and indiscriminate gunfire of the soldiers' attack. Skirmishers shot the camp dogs and scattered the meagre supplies of clothing and food. McKay made the most of the killing, then looked for decorated necklets and bags. He would sell most of them on as trophies of the so-called, Indian Wars. Gripping his sabre, Captain Pelt sat blood-crazed as his horse skittered and tripped among the cries of the dying Cheyenne. The Indians were defenceless, and within minutes the only sounds to be heard were those of the frightened dogs and horses. The only signs of movement, were ashy tendrils rising from trampled breakfast fires and burned tents.

★ ★ ★

After five days there was no obvious sign of a massacre, except for the unnatural and cruel appearance of a small stretch where the Indians had camped.

The soldiers from Fort Denton had returned to conceal the remains of their engagement. They were under orders, and with rakes and shovels they scoured the earth into bare runnels across shallow graves.

Among the company, there were two civilians. One was employed by Washington to act as a negotiator with the tribes of the Indian Territories, and the other who was a sutler. During the mass burial, the sutler, Rumer Wheat, in his desire for a native relic, lashed out with his boot at the attentions of a scavenger dog. He was after a blanket that had been decorated with strands of wolf hair and blue jay feather. He tugged the blanket and was astonished when he uncovered a small body lying in the cold grey ash. It was a pale-skinned Indian boy, no more than three years old, and he clawed silently at the ground in mute fear.

Wheat was instinctively on his guard, and he cautiously dragged the body closer to the stream towards some porcupine grass. He looked around for any sign of being observed, and then dispatched the child into a shallow at the base of the clump. He feigned an official looking task, and returned to his horse to stuff the Indian blanket into a pouch. He poured a handful of barley pellets into a raggedy army cap, and casually tossed it in the direction of the unknowing child. He would mention it to a woman acquaintance when they pulled into Lizard Wells in two or three days' time. That was the town that provided rest and recuperation for the company, where the troopers would picket and reprovision, before circling back north to Fort Denton.

★ ★ ★

Erma Flagg clucked her mule forward. She edged it nearer the clearing that was almost fifty miles from Horse Creek Lakes. The spot was how it had been described to her by Rumer Wheat, only now it was crawling with pariah dogs, sniffing and scratching across the barren ground. They were hideously thin with mange, the fur eaten away to raw skin, and in their frustration they were uselessly tearing at their own bodies. They were fearful and depraved, and mostly half crippled. She had got used to the human variety in Lizard Wells. To her, it was what God had intended — dick and ribs — the ape on nature. But this animal wildness always frightened her and made her skin crawl.

There was a cloying, fruity cut to the air, and Erma retched at the wisps of putrid gas that were already seeping through the earth. The mule balked and, as she turned its head away from the dogs, Erma caught sight of the vultures sweeping slowly in great circles less than a hundred feet above them. She spat contemptuously, and looked towards the stream through the clusters of grass. She found what she was looking for, and nudged the mule slowly across the soft, dipping ground. The scrawny child was kneeling in the shallow water, staring at the silver ripples as they weaved between the folds of his breech-clout.

From what Wheat had told her, the child had probably gone without food for at least five days. Since then, there had been another shelterless bout of survival on nothing but cress, water and a handful of army horse pellets. Her smile was genuine, but her sarcastic thoughts were for Rumer Wheat. In Erma, the sutler had identified her emptiness, but what she saw in front of her would hardly make life in Lizard Wells complete.

Erma cautiously climbed from the mule and stooped to pick up a crumpled, blue army cap. She reckoned it was the tenth day, and was already considering 'Moses' a fitting name for the halfbreed child.

6

Soon after the massacre, Ben Brooke moved far from the Indian Territories into the uninhabited snowline of the eastern Ozarks. He would use his anger and emptiness at the loss of his young family to forge a plan for his eventual return and retribution.

It was during the second or third year, late autumn, and he was hunting for meat. He was moving along his trapline, alert for a deer. His eyes were relaxed as they scanned the fresh, lightly drifting snow, then suddenly sharp, when a figure appeared stark against the drift of pure whiteness.

The body was half hidden under a pile of snow, but one arm was stitched along the barrel of a carbine that pointed almost straight at him. Ben fell into a crouch, and brought up his Navy Colt. He watched tensely for a few seconds before realizing something was wrong. The figure was too unmoving, too fixed. The hand that clawed the barrel was frosted and emaciated, and snow finely ridged the dark metal.

Ben waited for his pulse to drop, then he trudged closer and pushed aside the barrel. The movement toppled a ragged coonskin into the snow, and a blood-less, withered head fell sideways. Empty eye sockets glowered at him, and from half a jaw, a row of blackened teeth grimaced insanely.

The grisly tableau held Ben in a spasm of horror. He'd encountered many animals trapped in the frozen rictus, but this leering petrified human, caused his heart to race again. He lowered his Colt, and stared at the man hunched before him.

Shredded remnants of buckskin still adhered to one arm, traces of skin stretched like cloth across the back of the hand, white knucklebones gleamed. The other arm was missing, cut from the elbow. It was the after-death

Cheyenne sign, meaning death without honour.

Deerskin hung from lower, exposed parts of the corpse, and through one ragged legging, a white bone stuck into the drifted snow. He'd maybe been a trapper, a hunter. Ben wondered how long he'd crouched in the snow, while the seasons turned silently around him.

He stepped around the dead man, and kicked aside a mound of soft snow. He looked down, and saw a form of small, rough stones nestling in a crust of pine needles. It was a curious cluster, and he knelt to scrape away the pine.

He caught a movement from the corner of his eye, and whirled to see a baby pine-marten disappear into a thick tangle of icy bracken. He flinched, and turned back to the stones beside his knee. They'd been stored in a hide knife case which had long been eaten by land mites, and they weren't stones, but silver ore.

He put his head down to the snow, and looked into the tunnel the marten had formed. He put in his hand and drew out a handleless pick. He'd found the workings of a small silver lode.

Ben immediately understood. The man had been an opportune prospector. The seam was on Cheyenne land, and he'd put up a fight trying to retain what in fact he was stealing. That would explain the missing arm. It also told Ben how Long Moon acquired the silver he liked to trade. It would be unlikely that anyone else would ever find the small working — only the braves on a wide ranging forage.

He turned back to the corpse, and tugged at the ground vine around the lower legs. Rotten boot leather came away, and a heavy buckle fell from the shreds of a belt. It fell against a leg bone, and Ben jumped as the sound cracked the absolute silence of the snowline.

The first few prospectors to try their luck in the Cheyenne hills had returned with stories of silver running underfoot,

45

through the very grass, silver rivers that ran around the mountain walls. Many of the greedy bunch that trailed up to the Indian lands in pursuit of riches, paid an awful price for their killing ways and indiscriminate takeover.

It was approaching first dark, and from far off, Ben heard the call of the timber wolves. It was their territorial warning, and he took a last look around him. He rolled ore through his fingers, and smiled ruefully. He decided that over a period of time, it was probably what Long Moon had owed him with his sharp trade.

★　★　★

In Lizard Wells, a group of men sat in a clapboarded building that called itself 'hotel'. They wore uniforms of the US Cavalry.

Captain Gideon Pelt looked around the room and sniffed. 'No need to ask if McKay's here,' he sniggered.

One of four ragged troopers smiled

uncomfortably. 'Yeah, he's around some-place. You come to tell us what we're doin', Cap?'

Feet up on the table, Pelt took his time and lit another cheroot. 'What we're trained to do.'

Another trooper looked disconsolate and unsure. 'There ain't no more o' *that* sort o' doin' for any of us. We only been trained to take orders, an' there ain't no more o' that, either,' he said.

Lieutenant Ketchum looked severely at the trooper. 'That's right. You can try makin' your own way if you've a mind to, soldier.'

'We killed Injun under army orders ... *your* orders. We don't know nothin' else. How'd we get ourselves feed an' pay?' the trooper wanted to know.

At that moment, the scout, McKay appeared from an inside doorway. 'Well, it sure ain't goin' to be the army.' He turned to the sutler, Rumer Wheat. 'How 'bout you, Wheat? You must have somethin' stashed away after all them years of over-chargin', short measures

47

an' outright stealin'. How about we all divvy up?'

The sutler looked troubled and shifted uneasily in his chair.

Ketchum looked at the men around him. 'I say we find us a town without too much law, or maybe a town that needs it. You men don't need much more'n whiskey an' whores.'

Captain Pelt joined in. 'What do you say, sutler? There ain't much more profit to be made from the fort. Not unless you're thinkin' o' goin' into the charcoal business.'

Wheat got to his feet and brushed his hand across a filthy window. 'We can stay put. The sheriff ain't up to much, an' it's one o' the mail-line stages. We can even make trade with what's left o' them redskins.' The sutler glanced fleetingly at McKay, and the others sniggered at his cruel and sarcastic opportunism. 'They'll appreciate your kind o' negotiatin', or what happens if they don't,' he continued. 'We can use the stage line to carry pretty trinkets an' the like back to Jefferson. I'll stay on at Snake Pass. There'll be a steady stream o' them grubstakers, now the Injun trouble's mostly cleared up, an' protection from you an' your boys. We can stay here for ever, no need to change anythin'.'

'Yeah, I reckon you're on to somethin' there, Rumer.' Ketchum shared a disturbing, wily exchange with McKay and Pelt.

7

Erma Flagg was looking for Moses. It was late evening and he'd disappeared soon after they'd been sat jawing with their old friend, Osuno. But the boy hadn't gone very far. He was in the dark alley behind the saloon. It was a foul sodden gap, where men pissed away whiskey and vinegary beer.

He had one hand pressed flat against his buttocks, and his other hand clutched around his stalk. At eight years old, Moses made an impressive noise as his water splattered against the crusty planking.

Erma smiled thinly, and through the top of her old, well-worn army cap she scratched her head vigorously.

Moses sensed there was someone there, and half turned his head. He moved his free hand to the side of his leg, hissed and eased a skinning knife between his fingers.

A little reassured at finding him, Erma backed off and returned to her home ground of the saloon.

In five years, Lizard Wells had put nerve and temper into Moses, naturalized him into frontier law. He already possessed instinctive tools for survival, the singleness and observance of his mother, Blue Sky, the unyielding spirit of his father, Ben Brooke. From Osuno, the ageing, nomadic mountain man, he'd learnt about the skills of making, the ways of horses and use of weapons, even a little of Cheyenne culture and legend.

Osuno had brought a close-mouthed history to Lizard Wells. More than ten years earlier, he'd ridden in from Northern Wyoming, a crippled drifter, whose past was done with, and private. It was Erma who tended to his rehabilitation from a single bullet lodged deep in his side. He'd carried the internal damage for six weeks, and for hundreds of miles. No one ever recovered the bullet, but Osuno had reclaimed his fitness with food and rest, and then labour in the wagon yard and stables.

Osuno held a deep fascination for young Moses. Erma had told him that when the stranger arrived in Lizard Wells, he'd remained silent for days on end. She'd laughed, said it was what had first attracted her to him. When she'd asked him his name, he'd smiled and considered for a while before coming up with Osuno. And that's how it had stood. Erma had never known the whole truth about Osuno. But without query or slant she accepted it, passed the enigma on to young Moses.

Osuno didn't spend more than a few days in the town any more. He would disappear into the mountains for months on end, bringing back critters to trade off against whiskey, gambling and a pair of fresh mules.

★   ★   ★

The sun had already set when Erma reached the first broken strands of alder along the timberline. It was where the River Piney slithered from the trees, and not wanting to ride after dark, she decided to make her camp.

She tied her horse on a long rope, then went about making a blanket spread within reach of the water. She hadn't slept outside in a long while, and she'd ridden out too fast to gather much in the way of victuals. She had a strip of salted beef and some syrup peaches. Osuno was right when he'd said that if it wasn't for canned food, there wouldn't have been any settlin' west of the Mississippi.

It had also been a few months since she'd been on a long ride, and now she wondered about her mission. Moses' disappearance worried her, and she oughtn't to be chasing after him, not interfering with his quest, no matter how tragic. If he'd asked her, it would have been all right, but just watching, then chasing after him, wasn't.

Erma had been doing teach and tell, ever since she'd first lifted him from the ground. She lived in two rooms above the saloon, and for the last five years, had shared them with the boy. She'd clothed him, and taught him some rudiments, like how to sit at table — pass the peas. With Osuno's help, she'd taught him some letters, cipher and a dozen other white person things. But she couldn't touch the half of him that was needing more. The developing bit that sought involvement with his past and Cheyenne customs.

She rolled into her blanket and stared at the stars across the deep blue sky. In the morning she'd go back to town, leave the youngster to his Indian culture. Before sleep Erma's thoughts turned to Osuno. She wondered if he was playing the town, frequenting one of those tented whore-houses, playing cards, drinking, bragging about his knowledge of Indian tongue — his performance for a free jump. Her horse nickered and she raised her head. From

54

high in the timberline a lonesome dog-wolf howled. Then there was nothing, only the zizz of desert crickets, and she sighed into the snug of her camp.

8

The penetrating winds forged across Northern Missouri. The tawny leaves were edged with frost in the runs and arroyos, and the season's first streamers of snow lay white along the jagged mane of the Ozarks. There were hard, stubborn qualities to the land, and it reflected in the small herd of mustangs that grazed below the timberline. They were drifting to the nooks and pockets of the river breaks, where there was still grazing in the brome and rye grass.

It was cold, and Ben Brooke felt icy rivers of sweat running down his neck and across his shoulders. The silence was overpowering, and his heart thumped in fast aching spasms. He wouldn't move because an Appaloosa stallion was standing off the herd. It trotted stiff-legged to within thirty yards of where Ben crouched, arrogant in its ownership and command.

It raised its huge black head towards him, but Ben held every nerve tight. It was the Indian way of hunting, and he could remain that way for six hours if he had to.

The stallion's eyes were mean with challenge, and the inside of its flaring nostrils were swollen red, and gleaming. It curled its lips against huge yellow molars to let out one screaming whinny, and Ben crumpled. He had never felt such terror from a physical presence and, against all reason, he flung up his arms and yelled.

The stallion broke and whirled towards its small band of mares. They fled, running wildly in swerving files through the grass and low scrub. After a full mile, and with the mares in continuing flight, the stallion muscled itself into a dramatic, dustraising halt. He faced back towards Ben, stamping his forelegs and branding the hard ground with his fearful hoofs.

Ben pulled the cotton bandanna from his forehead and smeared a film of sweat and sand across his face. He spat, retied the damp fabric around his neck and walked slowly forward. The temperature was dropping fast, and he felt the cold, ripple through his body.

Ben kneeled and laid the palm of one hand against the chilly soil. He ran a finger around the rim of a hoof print and looked hard at the blanket of dust coiling low in the distance. He'd found his horse.

★   ★   ★

An hour passed, Ben had collected his thoughts, and the stallion was still visible. He'd made up his mind to go into the chase.

He went off at a steady lope, conserving his strength. It was the long distance endurance run of the tracking Indian. He cut between the stallion and the mares, giving the big Appaloosa something new to worry about. After two hours of unremitting chase, the stallion appeared to be tiring of its line, but it never slackened. They had run away from the setting sun, and when the last darkness finally came, the stallion was still resolute in its flight.

Ben had his blanket tied in a roll across his back. He found a shallow scrape, and curled on his side, his body outline just below the flat of the land. The night would layer down cold, but he was hardened to severe conditions.

As first light opened up, Ben stood and shook the frosty cut from his blanket. He looked out towards the stallion, smiled grimly and started into another run. They were still separated by a good mile, but twice during the morning Ben closed to within hundreds of yards.

Ben knew the time was approaching when he could make a move. He kneeled, looked west into the pale rising sun, and squeezed hard on a rawhide bolas that was once part of a Long Moon trade.

The stallion was now slightly less than a hundred yards ahead of Ben. It was fronting him, still alert, but looking wearied. Ben knew that the wild strength would return at the first sign of danger. The Appaloosa would fight like a demon in the face of capture.

The wintry sun was backlighting the stallion, and Ben couldn't take his eyes away. He hardly dared blink for fear the horse would be gone. He watched anxiously as it broke into a faltering trot through the packed mud that bordered the creek. Ben had his flask, but he knew the horse wouldn't go much further without a drink.

He took time, and worked himself downwind. He eased closer, taking cover advantage of tumbleweed and stunted jack pine. From across the creek, the stallion was nervous and made slight cries of anguish as it lowered its nose into the chilly water.

From forty feet, Ben knew it was the closest he would get. He raised himself, took one long back-swing and hurled the bolas low across the surface of the creek. He saw the whirling strips coil into the stallion, the hide pellets squeezing low around its big forelegs.

He scythed his way fast through the shallow creek, straight at the falling horse. It was already thrashing in an attempt to disentangle itself from the slice of the bolas. Ben threw himself on to the big, wild head. He forced the stallion's ears to the ground, locking the fingers of his right hand under the horse's jaw. He drew the great black muzzle towards him, pulling and twisting the gleaming neck into his body. The stallion continued to struggle and lash out with his hind feet, and Ben felt a wild blast from its nostrils heat the side of his face. He hung on, bracing every muscle against the pull of the Appaloosa.

They lay in the desert sand for an hour, and as Ben felt an ebb of the stallion's struggle, his hands and leg muscles relaxed a little. It was a crucial moment, and he cautiously began to free one of his hands. He untied his bandanna and laid it across the big fearful eyes, then unwound a knotted cord from around his waist. He worked it under and over the stallion's head, tentative and easy, taking care not to release too much pressure. He made the cord into a slip-noose and worked it through the long, thick black mane.

When the stallion climbed to its feet, there'd be trouble, and Ben would be in a vulnerable position. A strike from any hoof would be lethal. He set himself hard against the renewed pulling of the horse's head. If it got its nose and powerful neck free, Ben would join the big mozzies that clouded the banks of the creek.

Ben's shoulders and arms were beginning to spasm with strain. Every time he loosened his hold, even a little, the stallion sensed it and immediately renewed its pressure. It would be a long and debilitating contest. Ben didn't know whether he could hold out or not, and once again, first dark was approaching. He was hungry now, his water was finished and he felt numbness creeping through him.

He felt a tremble through the stallion's neck, instinctively released his hold. The stallion rolled, snorted wildly and surged upward. The bolas had loosened, and it dropped away from the stallion's front feet. The lunge almost lifted Ben clear of the ground, and he clung on in desperation. The stallion leaped forward in a frantic bucking run, shaking his head and squealing, swinging wide against Ben's sweat-soaked arms. The rope was hanging free, and they were off running. Ben was dragged, the toes of his skin boots stabbing furrows across the flats.

After several hundred yards, the stallion knew it wasn't gaining freedom. It powered into a sudden check, swinging Ben ahead of its stand. Ben's heart was pounding with elation or terror, he didn't know which. He fought to gain his footing. He was breathless, but managed to wheeze Cheyenne incantations into the stallion's ear. He'd forgotten the meanings, but he hoped they'd influence the tiring horse. His voice was cracked and shaking with emotion.

The tension was flowing away, and Ben took hold of the rope, just below the stallion's great jowls. Then he let his fingers slip, slow but deliberate until he had a six foot lead. He tugged gently on the rope, and laughed in amazement. By the open movement, he'd offered the stallion its freedom.

Ben let the end of the rope trail away. He walked exhausted back to the creek, staring at the ground ahead of him. He saw the wavering shadow move alongside, then the stallion's nose nudged him between his sagging shoulder blades. In letting the horse have a choice, he'd made the first move of a lasting alliance.

9

Far into the timber, Moses crouched silent and watchful. He was twelve now and, as a half-breed he'd not counted coup for that part of his blood. He'd divested his boots and jacket, cached them at the furthest outskirts of Lizard Wells. He wore the simple skin leggings of a Cheyenne buck.

He listened to the murmuring of the Piney as it ribboned its way down through the timberline. Every so often it pooled into small lakes for fishing and beaver trapping. Once into the Breaks, the river broadened and meandered towards two or three isolated townships, then the tributaries of the Mississippi.

He caught a flick of movement through a pine stand. It was the merest flash of a rider who'd moved too far from the trees. It would be Sinoca and his paint, riding brazen and headstrong. A year ago he'd made friends with Sinoca while fishing a lake inside Indian Territory. But Sinoca was a Kiowa, and Moses was from the Cheyenne, and Kiowa braves didn't even like each other. Fortunately, the boys were of similar age, and rawness afforded them a shared vision of their predicaments.

Moses gripped his skinning knife and hissed through his teeth, but it was a few minutes before he caught sight of Sinoca again. He was close, out from the pine, and he trotted his pony haughtily towards Moses.

Moses looked up to the young Kiowa. 'I saw you from the furthest lake.'

'I hope the bluecoats did too.' Sinoca leapt to the ground, and stretched on the soft pine needles and bracken. He peered down towards the lakes. 'One day more.'

'How many of them?' Moses asked.

Sinoca held up the fingers of one hand. 'Seven or eight. The Dead Meat leads them.'

To the youngsters, no one was more odorous and cursed than The Dead Meat, the man the bluecoats and Moses knew as McKay. He stole beaver and fox from the Indians' traps, and brought them to Lizard Wells for trade. He was a killer of both Kiowa and Cheyenne. Even the bloodthirsty Arapaho put out their arms to him. McKay's strength was his natural cruelty. Moses shuddered, then thought about his approaching coup.

Sinoca was half dozing, still enough to feel the katydids that flicked his outstretched fingers. 'What is this medicine you will steal from The Dead Meat?' he asked. He knew it wasn't a pony. The Cheyenne traded with the Pawnee for better horse flesh than any white-man trapper owned. It wasn't a pistol or rifle. The Cheyenne had killed Arapaho and Shawnee for guns, long before other whites had come to the mountains. And it wouldn't be found in a bag or pocket. Moses and Sinoca had already plundered dead trappers' grips, but found no great medicine. For

Moses, there wasn't much that couldn't be gained or found in the town he lived in.

Moses stood up and walked to the feet of Sinoca. 'It is something that he carries close. He wears it next to his skin.'

'Ha! You're going to steal his stinkin' drawers?' Sinoca laughed, but there was no response from Moses. His mind was already elsewhere.

Together they rode along the river bank to a cut. It was where the bluecoats and McKay would pass on their way through the lakes.

Moses took a broken Shawnee hunting lance from a tuck in his saddle blanket. He looked at Sinoca, nodded, and placed a finger in the top of his left shoulder. It was going to be his effort for mercy when the bluecoats found him.

Sinoca pulled his pony in close and looked hesitantly at Moses. 'There's many hours before they get here,' he said.

'If the blood runs thin, they'll start looking for the Shawnee who did it,' Moses' chest was heaving, and he pushed the lance at Sinoca. 'There's some in your tribe wouldn't find it so difficult. Do it now.'

The innate tribal rivalry ran close to the surface. Sinoca quickly took the lance, grinned viciously and drove the thin blade deep into Moses' shoulder.

The young half-breed ground his teeth in pain, then turned his horse. He rode into a deep, split outcrop to wait for the bluecoats and The Dead Meat. The lance twisted with the horse's trot, tearing its blade through the flesh of his tortured shoulder.

He didn't try to pull the lance while Sinoca was close. He waited until he heard him ride away, back into the Kiowa territory. The point of the lance had locked into his shoulder bone, and the pain made him irrational and weak. He smelled the sweat, and felt the salt running into his eyes.

He sat in the shallows of the stream,

under the outcrop, and clamped his teeth around the short, broken shaft of the lance. He gripped his fingers around the bloody wound, and with one neck wrench, he drew the point away. The pain was so great, the trees and sky turned white, then silver, then black with moons and shooting stars.

Moses' horse nosed inquisitively at the inert body, then galloped down to the Breaks, back in the direction of Lizard Wells.

When Moses regained his consciousness, hours had passed and he was shivering in the shallow water of the stream. His shoulder was on fire with pain, and he pushed damp moss into the wound. Then he climbed slowly onto the bank and lay exhausted in the thick, soft grasses.

During the ensuing night, he was tortured, delirious, and many dreams came to him. He heard the sounds of gunfire, screaming and barking dogs. He saw the ghosts of people wreathed in smoke, then it was pitch black again, and he thought he was dead.

The night was long, and eventually, when grey light seeped through the pines, he warily took a drink from the stream. Then he climbed on to the bank and curled in tight to the base of the outcrop. For five hours he hid, burning with thirst. It was mid-morning when he heard the noise of horse rigging, and he crawled from his lair onto the low bank of the stream. He lay gaunt and pale, awaiting the bluecoats and McKay.

★　★　★

They sat solidly in their saddles. Two of them sniggered, and McKay lowered his carbine towards Moses' body. 'He's a queer-lookin' Injun. Looks like a 'breed, an' that's a Shawnee wound.' The scout recognized the bloodied, iron lance point. It was lying on a small boulder in the middle of the stream.

Moses pushed himself resolutely to his feet. He faced up to them, fearless and eager. His ghostly dreams were exorcised. These men were real and, if they wanted to, they'd kill him. He ground his teeth and hissed.

The Dead Meat, McKay, dismounted and shoved him back to the ground. Moses would have fought him there and then, but he'd already seen the medicine. It was the coup he was seeking; a small skin pouch, decorated with blue and yellow beads. The Cheyenne treasure bag was hanging low around the scout's neck.

Moses recognized the uniformed soldier who came riding up. He carried a sword and two pistols strapped across his chest. He was the leader of the bluecoats that rode from Lizard Wells. When he said things, others minded his words. The man eased himself down from his horse.

'Must be a Cheyenne 'breed, Cap'n,' McKay said. 'Can't think why, but he looks kind o' familiar.'

Captain Gideon Pelt looked inquisitively at Moses.

Another bluecoat dismounted and pointed his revolver down at Moses' distressed face.

'No,' the captain said. Then he laughed. 'He's holdin' a lot back. It looks to me like he wants you to shoot him.'

'It's what we want. Kill him now,' McKay directed his vicious words at the captain.

Four more of the group rode up. They were leading the pack mules for trade with Arapaho and Kiowa. One of the riders leaned down to look close at the broken lance point. He dribbled a long strand of dark spittle into the stream, then twisted round to the captain and McKay.

'Cap'n Pelt,' he said. 'Why don't we ride on? In anyone's book, this here's a kid. It's a sad thing to waste time over, even for us. With respect, Cap'n.'

McKay was searching his memory, glaring down at Moses. The scout's cold eyes didn't waver, and he spoke to no one in particular. 'He's some sort o' button, all right, but given half a chance, he'll eat your liver.'

The bluecoat who'd looked at the lance turned to McKay and grinned. 'The Shawnee will more'n likely take good care of him. We know they ain't too friendly with his sort, an' they won't be too far from one they already got wounded.'

Moses looked up at Pelt. He knew they wouldn't harm him until the captain gave the word. Moses saw a thin, almost guilty looking smile flit across the man's face as he stepped his horse over him.

'Put him on a lead. Perhaps he's worth somethin' to somebody,' he said.

Moses now walked with hunger gnawing inside him, but his legs were strong. The riders' horses kicked up dirt, and it crusted in the thin painful sweat that ran down his body. He'd stay quiet and self-possessed, though.

After a six-hour trek across the timberline, the group approached Arapaho land. They returned later with their loads intact, but they brought back fur, skins and Indian gewgaws. One of the troopers waved a switch of skin and hair, and Moses knew they hadn't made a trade. They'd killed another small band and, in fear of retribution, set out a night guard.

In the failing light, McKay was looking at Moses, and talking to one of the troopers. 'We're jus' storin' up trouble here. That hatred's goin' to grow. Them 'breeds got special powers.'

Moses decided he had to get his medicine quickly and make his coup. It was going to be difficult, the scout never took the pouch from his body. He hardly ever seemed to sleep, and never took a wash outside of his clothes. Often the scout saw Moses watching, and it troubled him. He knew who Moses was singling out.

The bluecoats were eating around their campfire, and Moses was rolled into a blanket. But he was nowhere near sleep.

It was very late when at last his

opportunity came, when he saw McKay rolling himself into a buffalo skin. He waited for another hour, then, draped in his blanket, he went to sit near the fire. The night picket was toasting small pieces of meat and, as Moses walked softly towards him, he made the slightest nod of recognition. Moses smiled innocently, let some pain be seen, as he crouched alongside the man. His left arm hurt badly as he held out his hand towards the warmth of the fire, but with his right, he gently teased a hunting knife from the man's leg sheath. The man turned to Moses, almost as if he knew what was happening and smiled again. The smile remained, then increased before turning into a shallow grimace as the knife blade sliced quick and deep across his throat.

Moses rolled the man's body into a heap, quietly, as it expired of its life. There was a low, gurgling sound, but for no more than a few seconds. Moses looked around him, and across the clearing saw that McKay was still asleep and snoring.

The gleam from the flames caught the bright beads of the Cheyenne treasure bag, and Moses made a thin, hissing sound. Across the soft bed of pine needles he crawled in close to the army scout. Using the dead soldier's knife, he gently cut the sinewed thong from around the scout's neck, backing slightly as he caught the overwhelming odour. He leaned over the sleeping man and mimicked the Cheyenne arm cut. But McKay was alive, hadn't yet died with dishonour, and Moses eased the bloody knife into the earth. As he wriggled silently away, he remembered Osuno once telling him to wash, because, 'Injuns could be smelled out by white men from more'n ten mile'. In Moses' case, it would be about five, he'd said, and they'd laughed.

★   ★   ★

On foot, it took Moses two days to get back to Lizard Wells. He jogged down through the pine, across the mountain streams and round the stands of alder that lined the beaver lakes. The fresh moss was effective on the wound in his shoulder, the medicine of the treasure bag had supported him, and he'd made his coup. At the end of the first day of his escape, he'd heard, then seen the troop. They were behind him, and they too were making their descent from the timberline back to town.

*　*　*

Erma had caught part of the story from two of the troopers outside the hotel. She'd already found the small horse standing near the livery stable, but knew instinctively, that it was Moses whom they'd been talking about. It wasn't just another of the boy's sudden disappearances. For Erma, the worry was heartfelt, and she'd had to come to terms with it. During the last few years there'd been no more trailing the youngster, no more following-on while he sought involvement with his ancestry. Although she didn't want to believe it, it sounded to Erma as though Moses had maybe started to piece together the grim story of Horse Creek Lakes.

10

Osuno was lying flat out, on a gently rising bluff. He was almost two miles north of Snake Pass, looking towards the overnight stage-stop. He'd crossed a narrow Indian trail earlier in the day. It was on the long, isolated dog-leg from Sedalia and, out of curiosity, he'd been tempted to follow. He wanted to know which of the tribes were still on the prod. He looked closely at the disturbed ground and estimated there were about a dozen warriors.

For fifteen years Osuno had tried to settle. Lizard Wells had provided a manner of refuge, but during the last few years he'd become more dissatisfied with the town and its oppressive regime. He returned four or five times a year to see Erma and Moses, but for the most part he stayed clear, moving between the Breaks and the timberline.

To the tribes of the Ozarks, he became one of the few sufferable buckskinned figures. To others, a curious private man, a throwback as the grabbers moved ever westward.

Under the guise of protecting commercial interests, the army had meted out their own harsh discipline against tribes within the Indian Territories. But some of the tribes were enraged, vengeful, and they fought back. Any isolated building without the close protection of army or a town, was in danger of attack at that time. If Osuno's instinct was right, he had followed the trail of a rebellious Cheyenne war party. Even at that distance he felt the cold sweat of unease about what was ahead.

For a while, he watched a plume of dark smoke coil its way up to a lone, circling vulture. He looked around, then carefully edged his way below the crest of the bluff to where his mule was standing. He climbed into the saddle and slowly worked his way towards the pass.

The smell of burning drifted in as he turned upwind within sight of the staging-post. The roof of the low building was gone, and charred beams angled into the sky. A stone chimney rose from the pile of smouldering embers where the timbers of one corner had completely burned away. He nudged his mule forward, his Winchester out of its scabbard and held ready across the horn of his saddle.

He stopped beside the corral rails and noticed the beaten-up ground where the horse teams had milled to get out. For a full minute he listened, but there was no sound other than the crackle of searing wood. He looked at the blackened, smoking ruins that had included the relay house and sutler's store. Torn sacks, dime-novels, and empty whiskey bottles were scattered by the walls, and yards of bright coloured fabric flapped around posts that had once held a door.

He dismounted wearily and walked around the corner of the building. There was no sign of any other person except the sutler. Rumer Wheat was sitting in a big oak chair, the only piece of furniture untouched by the fire. There were gouges in the soil that the legs had made when it had been dragged from the store.

On the ground were the scales with which the sutler had weighed out sweatmeats for travellers using the Dog Leg Stage. In his lap, the buckled pan held his arm that had been severed at the elbow.

Wheat's legs and neck had been tied to the chair. He hadn't been scalped, but his eyes were bulging, and they stared sightlessly at Osuno. His head was full to bursting too. His mouth had been stuffed with the corner of a blanket that had been decorated with wolf hair and blue-2 jay feather. The vengeance of the Cheyenne was wide, and they carried with them memories of Horse Creek Lakes.

There wasn't much Osuno could do, save cover up the sutler with the remainder of the blanket. The braves wouldn't be back, and the vulture wasn't alone any more. But the ground was too hard for digging, and he was too old and, if the truth be told, too disinclined. Among the ashes he found a broken jar and helped himself to a twist of warm tobacco. He turned a crate and sat in the shade of his mule. He'd spent a few years avoiding the bad doings that plagued the Indians of the Ozarks. For the Cheyenne, there were old scores, and some of them were still being settled.

Osuno was fifty miles out of Lizard Wells. He'd be returning south-east and away from the trouble. He reckoned he'd be safe enough, but it was still a long day's journey that he wouldn't finish until noon the following day.

★   ★   ★

Erma heard Osuno clumping up the steps to her room. The door was open to encourage any air that might relieve the oppressive heat. She nodded her head, and Osuno walked in with a rolled package he let fall to the floor.

'Where you been now, you silly old fool?'

'Snake Pass.'

'What in hell's name's out there of any interest to you?'

'I followed an Indian trail to Wheat's store.'

'Did you see him? How was he?'

'Well, he won't be feelin' the cold no more.'

Erma got up from where she was sitting and found her second chair for Osuno.

'I'll stay on me feet. Ain't much in a sittin' mood,' he declined.

'Was it the Cheyenne found him?' she asked.

'Yeah. They knew of him. Known for ten year, I guess.'

'You're sure it was Cheyenne, Osuno?'

Osuno moved further away from the chair. 'Oh yeah, I'm sure. Maybe one day I'll tell you why.'

'I thought we were finished with all that,' Erma said gloomily.

'I reckon we are now, Erma.'

Erma got up from her chair again. 'The sutler did manage to do one good thing in his life, anyways. I'll make you some coffee.'

Osuno grunted friendly like. 'How much money you got, Erma?' he asked.

'That's easy. Enough to last me 'til I get some more. An' that ain't much. You come back to rob me?'

'Nope. It's just that if you ever get to wantin' to leave here, I could grubstake you. I thought now was maybe the time to mention it.' Osuno dragged up the parcel. 'I'm in a generous mood,' he said, 'I brought you back a present.' He pulled out the end of a coloured roll of fabric. 'Maybe you can make somethin' pretty out o' this . . . a dress for someone.'

Erma caught the reflection of Osuno in her mirror. He was watching her, almost smiling.

'I sure will, if I ever get to see someone,' she replied, almost smiling at the sting of her own joke.

11

Ben Brooke cautiously led his stallion along the low mountain ridge. He whispered encouragement as the horse snickered and trembled its way through the shifting scree.

Across the rough peaks of the Ozarks, a dense metallic sky crushed down, and the sun rose higher as an immense brazen disc. It singed Ben's skin, and seared his lungs. He pinched his bandanna up close around his nose, as bleached dust powdered over him. His sweat ran as tiny threadlike rills into the pits and creases of his skin. The bridle reins were constantly slipping through the soapy wetness of his hands, and his eyes stung from salt.

They would never reach Lizard Wells by nightfall. He'd set one more camp before the Big Piney breached its banks and spilled into the vast plain of the

Missouri Breaks.

As night crept through the wilderness, Ben and his horse were down to the swift torrent. It was clean and inviting, and almost without the stallion knowing he was in the saddle, slapping them into a slow, soothing ride before bedtime. They walked in a wide circle, cooling in the silent breezes that brushed off the surface of the river.

There was young clover and snake bunny in the summer grasses, and Ben dismounted to ease off the broad belly girdle. The horse's muscles quivered, and its dappled coat glistened in the darkness as it pawed the rich soft earth. When the horse was satisfied, they moved to a rocky crossing where the water was shallower. Ben stood back and grinned at the violent snorting of his horse. It was startled at the sudden grip of chilly water that sluiced up and around its hot nostrils.

An hour later, after nearing the end of his supplies with a jack-rabbit stew, Ben made himself easy, with his back firmly bolstered in the curve of his saddle. He drew a blanket around him, laid his head back and looked directly up into inky blue darkness.

He could hear his stallion nosing inquisitively in the ground elder. His fire crackled gently, and flicked up tiny fragments of white ash. He crooked one arm loosely around his old Navy Colt. There was no holster, it was simply wound in a deerhide sash. His other arm was more cautious and rested on the stock of a Springfield rifle. Its long, heavy barrel was threaded through the loops of a rugged, canvas saddle pouch. It contained small coin, and his payload of a thousand dollars worth of silver ore.

★　★　★

In the early morning Ben woke to the fresh, biting cold. Spread out below him were the Breaks, 20,000 square miles of virgin hinterland, stretching from St. Louis to the Arkansas border. His horse was standing near, watching him, his great head bathed in a cloud of spiralling steam. Between dusk and dawn, there were sharp temperature swings in the low foothills. They didn't retain the diffused warmth of the plains, or the spiked frost of the high peaks. Ben fixed a short rope lunge, and cantered his horse to stir their circulations and revitalize taut muscles.

He sat in the lee of a spreading alder, and let his horse gently drag the lunge cord through his fingers. It backed away very slowly, its withers rippling with the carefully controlled movement. They enjoyed the play. It was a mutual demonstration of their freedom, but neither of them would be going separate ways out of choice.

The solitary customs of ten years were almost settled for Ben Brooke. Where there had once been great wildernesses, there were now expanding trails of settlers, businessmen and property speculators. Those native and genuine to the land were in conflict with the thoughtless advance that brought greenhorns and their hostile cultures.

Nearing forty, Ben had seen and suffered from its coming. It had been near the end of the Indian wars, alongside Horse Creek Lakes, that he'd lost his wife and child.

★ ★ ★

Ben had only seen the site of where the small band had met their deaths. The army had razed the killing ground in fear of its mistake; the unremitting retribution from 2,000 Cheyenne, Kiowa and Pawnee warriors.

For a year after, the east-west trails from Missouri to Kansas were closed. Through spring and summer and the following winter, Long Moon and Yellow Cloud's revenge war had continued. Fort Denton had been burned to the ground, but only after those soldiers responsible for the massacres had been discharged. They were the small company of military freebooters that now forged an existence out of the town of

Lizard Wells. Apart from the rare fur trapper, the Ozarks remained inalienably Indian. For Ben Brooke, it was the end of an era. For a decade he'd used the frozen wasteland in an attempt to cauterize the grief for his lost family.

But now he was ten or twelve hours from Lizard Wells and felt uneasy. It was a stark, crude town with prospectors, Indian traders and hunters who carried the old ways with them in their traps and holsters. Like him, they'd become too crusty and detached for social compromise or settlement.

Most important to Ben, it succoured the remnant soldiers of Fort Denton. The officers and troopers who'd never given up their soldiering and killing ways of the Indian Wars. They'd combined with deserters to live off their wits and threat of joint guerrilla engagement.

*　*　*

By the time Ben was ready to start the final unhurried descent into the Breaks, a clear orange glow was spreading up from the eastern horizon. It was unfamiliar territory, and the dawn air was filled with fresh stimulating fragrances. Some drifted in from the baked surfaces of the red earth, some from the tree blossom and basket grasses that lined the splintered streams of the Piney. Some were feral scents emerging from the desolate scrubland, but the most worrying were those drifting through almost unnoticed from Lizard Wells. It was those that the horse tested uneasily and for some time, before returning to play with his rig and empty oat sack.

Ben called him, and he came halfway over, still chewing on the crumpled remains of the feed bag. He tossed it high in the air, snorted loudly and whammed it with a front hoof. He stepped ostentatiously, and held up his head for approval. He was eager and ready, and within ten minutes Ben had him loosely snaffled and ready to move out.

They faced the expanse ahead of them, watching the land take shape in the early light. One rest around noon and they would make town by early evening. Ben mounted and eased the horse forward gently through the rocky edges of the foothills.

After a watchful hour, they finally stepped out onto the flat, earthed plains, and Ben moved the eager stallion from a walk into a full unrestrained gallop. There was no exertion or reaching for speed, it was simply notching up, enjoying the moving and exhilaration of restrained power. Ben felt the huge muscles pulsing under him and the miles eased away under the flying hoofs. Each hour he allowed the horse a drink and kick stomp in one of the streams that fanned out across the plain. They were the headwaters of the mighty Mississippi, the start of a thousand-mile journey.

Near midday, they called a halt beneath the shadows of cholla stand. The sun was at its fiercest, and its heat beat up from the ground in a heavy, shimmering vapour. Ben had some dried fruit in his pocket and he held out a few small pieces for his horse. He made himself a half-pint of coffee to stave off the gnawing. He boiled it in a can pushed into a handful of flaming animal chips and brush.

Another hour and Ben pulled up on the horse's cinch. He looked across the saddle into the vast landscape beyond. It was still four hours away, but he could sense and almost smell the town.

He yelled at his horse, and they took to the plain, scattering rabbits and quail from their mesquite hiding. They maintained an easy pace, and kept to the contours of one of the streams that would take them close.

The roughness of the country had softened, and they rode into an endless landscape devoid of edge or focus. The bare earth held only enough moisture to support patches of thorn and scrub grass, but ahead of them sucking out life was Lizard Wells.

Within three or four miles of the township, he could make out the shuffling outlines of clustered buildings. It was early evening, but everything still shimmered in the continuing heat of the land.

He jiggled the reins, twisted gently with his legs to swing the horse around. They stopped and stood sideways on, a private last minute gesture of their capability to take another direction, or go back. Ben then swung the horse forward, and he saw the whiteness of his knuckles, taut against the flesh of his fists.

12

It was five o'clock when they trotted into the south end of the town. The horse faltered momentarily as a small boy raced too close across the narrow street. Ben smiled coldly as the youngster dragged a live water moccasin through the dust. It was tied by the tail to a long length of string, and he had a friend running behind, lashing its writhing body with a thick switch of willow.

Ben had seen a nest of the snakes earlier in the day. They had been disturbed by his horse stamping around in a muddy hollow. He'd panicked with revulsion at the brown slithering coils, and heeled the stallion anxiously away to the safety of hardbaked earth. He shivered at the memory, and instinctively made soft encouraging noises as they walked further down the street. He was looking for army signs, but to any watching eyes, Ben appeared uninterested in the people and their assorted mongrel buildings.

The ground dropped slightly ahead of them, and Ben was aware of his presence being followed from the raised board sidewalks. On a nearby roof he noticed someone fixing a crude weathervane, and whoever it was stopped to watch them pass. All the buildings appeared temporary by their distressed appearance and makeshift construction. To a stranger the town offered cold-harbour stations, with no visible comforts or trade. That was all right with Ben though. He didn't require either.

A mangy, grey dog suddenly sprang from under a sidewalk step and snapped viciously at the underbelly of his horse. Ben looked directly into the spiteful, yellow eyes and placed his hand on the stock of his Springfield. From where it was set in its scabbard, he could have fired an ounce bullet straight down through the roof of the dog's skull. He spoke more reassuring words and shied away.

They stood reserved in the hard-packed dirt of the narrow street, and Ben glanced at the muddled selection of buildings. At the bare, wagon yard end, where he first set foot, and the northern end with its scattering of dreary single-storey clapwood dwellings, whiskey barrels for chimneys and sacks for windows. In front of him was the quarter that incorporated a miners' bank and a sheriff's office. To the side of that was a blacksmith's shop and a two-storey livery stable.

Behind him, and set back from the street was an area that he sensed, rather than had knowledge of. He turned and cast an eye over the tents and ramshackles that provided entertainment for outcasts of the Breaks. It was a lair of prostitution, gambling and gunplay for mavericks and renegades, part of an isolated frontier, where law and order came second to survival.

He nudged the horse forward, and

they crabbed up to the livery stable. It seemed a fitting moment to get fodder, water and a grooming for the stallion, and he slowly dismounted and looked for signs of a liveryman. They walked into the stable and he was immediately stung by the acrid saturation of horse sweat and soiled hay. In one corner was a large pile of buffalo skins. Next to it were several stacks of dried meat, and the soft pelts of smaller animals. There was a crate with two grizzly cubs, and another with two young wolves. They were orphaned by the fur trade, were awaiting an arduous journey to Boston or New York. For eastern city dwellers it was living confirmation of a primitive world at the wild frontier. Standing in one wretched stall was a rib mule that chewed aggressively at its rope bridle. It flicked its long ears back, shot both forelegs into a thick crust of its own manure. Ben was grateful for the crude wooden slat that partially closed the pen, and he hauled the stallion's nose protectively in close above his shoulder. The wolf pups were asleep and snuffling softly.

The bear cubs were curled securely in their crates but wide awake. Their dark jowls were collapsed to the floor, but their eyes moved from side to side at a terrifying world. As Ben backed through the open gates they raised their heads and looked at him accusingly. He pushed hard at his horse's shoulder, and turned sharply away from the building. He moved them at a trot back in the direction of the saloon he'd passed earlier.

Daylight was fading fast, and one or two pale flickering lights were already appearing through cracks along the street front. Except for the occasional crude sign, the flat-fronted buildings were featureless. The River Bend Saloon had two dusty windows, and rusting metal characters that spelled out BAR, were nailed to one side of its single door. Ben wrapped a strap of rein around a hook on the other side, looked at his horse and nodded at the loose tether. It was a mere gesture of restraint. That way, at least one of them was going to be halfway out of trouble. He slung his saddle pouch over his shoulder, stamped his feet and laid the palm of his hand against the Navy Colt. It was hanging on a hide sash around his neck, tucked and hidden within the flap of his long, doeskin coat. He took another look at his horse, glanced up and down the dreary street and entered the bar.

The exterior, disguised the recently constructed inner shell of a room. It was lined and floored with green pine, and together with the mingled aromas of tobacco and oaked whiskey, was curiously favourable. There were five or six tables, and each one had a fat tallow candle sitting in the centre, but like the world outside, everything appeared to be dust-caked and colourless.

Ben walked unhurriedly to one end of bar, where a long mirror and a wall clock, had recently been installed. He surveyed the unlikely looking stock, and asked the barkeep for a beer. He guessed it might be a mistake, changed his mind and settled for whiskey. He lifted a hard-boiled egg from a wooden bowl, bit off the top and dipped the bright yolk into the fearsome spirit. It was a few years since he'd taken a shot of raw booze, and he wasn't prepared to exhibit the fact. For anyone interested enough, this was how he took his food. He stared into the mirror behind the bar, then the counter for a minute or so. He shuffled the sawdust about at his feet and took an oblique look around the room. He took just enough interest in the few occupied tables to discount the show of soldier blue, that caught his eye.

* * *

Down the street, there were only four men in the hotel. Two of them were the remainder of Captain Gideon Pelt's Company, and they sat in thoughtful, worried conversation.

'It's months since I seen a whole dollar,' one of them said. 'Them whores'll only give so much on a handshake. An' another thing, I want to keep me liver.'

'Hell, *that* ain't the organ those cats are interested in,' the corporal said, and guffawed.

'Not *them*. It's an Injun, I'm talkin' about. That 'breed kid. The one that just about severed Jenkle's head. You remember him?'

'Yeah, I remember him. He could o' done us all that night. But so what?'

'He's here in town. I seen him outside o' the hotel. He's feathered out some . . . wearin' what looks like store-boughts, but it's him all right. McKay said we shoulda skinned him.'

'Huh. Maybe it's him, maybe it's not. Best not to sleep for too long though.'

'I think we should move on. Further west, to the other side o' the Ozarks. Kansas maybe. I hear it's rich, plenty there for the takin'.'

'There's plenty for the takin' right

here in the tents.'

'Get a goddam tune out o' that pianer,' a drunk shouted, and the trooper looked up.

The hotelier moved irritated off his couch and slammed his fingers across the stained, beaten keys.

The trooper turned back to his one-time corporal. 'There's somethin' else 'bout this place that ain't good. I've felt it for some time. You noticed, the coach ain't runnin' through anymore?'

'You goin' to tell Pelt about your misgivins'?' the corporal asked, looking curiously at the trooper. 'You know he don't take kindly to deserters.'

'I thought about it. Thought I'd tell you first. Thought maybe you'd want to come.'

'Well, I can tell you gave it some thought.' The corporal winked slyly. 'But if I did come, there'd be less chance for you an' them rich pickin's.' The corporal looked about him. 'Guess I'll hang around here for a while longer. If there's anyone left in this flea-bed, we

can eat, then go take care o' the horses.'
He laughed at his own unpleasantness,
shouted across at the piano player.
'Get some food an' some light in this
place.'

13

Having only two small front windows, all the candles in the River Bend were now well alight. Two men were sitting feet up, with their heels resting on a circular brass bar around the open top of a pot-bellied stove. Against the near wall, an old man with a beaver hat let the front legs of his chair thump to the floor. He was still fast asleep, but it aroused the attention of the three other people who were sitting at another table. One of them was Moses, and his partner was a young hunchback named Curly Page. The third was Erma Flagg. She was the one wearing a Yankee cavalryman's cap and baggy navy breeches. There was one glass and a half-finished bottle of whiskey.

Curly was born with a twisted body, a rejected outcome of the whorehouses; another who'd been offered a semblance of childhood by Erma. Inexplicably, she'd never considered a second name for Moses. But for Curly, Page was a word from the only book she'd ever read. The confines of Lizard Wells had provided Curly and Moses with common ground. They'd fought before, but childish affairs, when youngsters taunted affliction and difference. It was only during their adolescent years that an uneasy alliance began to fester.

They were timekilling, ribbing and playing cards with Erma. The game was an obvious catalyst for their frustrations, and Curly was pushing it with sneers and torment. ''Breeds ain't got no place . . . bit like a dumb accident from a horse'n donkey. Hee haw . . . hee haw.'

Moses had been ready. He'd sensed it growing for some time. They both knew and accepted that that moment might as well be the time and place.

Curly glanced at Erma, then smirked at Moses. He made his customary scuffle from the table, then made a deceptive sideways movement to cross the floor of the saloon. Fronting up to any watchers, it minimized the tortured shape of his back, but to those who knew him, it deepened his unease and suffering. Erma's face chilled, as Moses followed. She didn't look at him; she knew he didn't want her to. It was verging on man's stuff, the priority of a fist as a message.

Curly hopped the gap from the saloon floor to the ground. The outside steps had passed through the final stages of decay, and all that remained were the rusty iron rivets. It was three hours past midday, and the trapped air of the alleyway was oppressive and massively stifled. Curly felt the inside of his gummy collar, and dragged at the tight jacket of his suit. He watched Moses, ridiculed his name, and edged along the side of the saloon until they stood close in the deep, musty shadows. They opened with garbled slurs, standing on ground that was furrowed and edged like the crusting of pies. The sun hardly reached the gaps between the crowded wood structures, and the putrid excrescence from the saloon spread foul puddles around their feet.

Curly started to undo the front of his trousers. It was with his left hand and awkward, but a cheat for what he did next. His right hand suddenly swung round from the side, aiming for the beak of Moses' face. It was meant to be one punch, not a fight, but Moses had sensed the movement, and before it plugged in, he sidestepped and Curly stumbled forward. He was temporarily off balance, and Moses ripped a quick blow into his head. It was vicious, and cracked Curly's nose, spurting flecks of dark blood across his face. Curly snorted and his legs buckled, but he managed to gurgle some air in and out of his face.

His eyes were eager and glaring, and Moses quickly hit him again. It was meant as a sharp finisher, and his knuckles welded into Curly's mouth. It was like striking pebbles and he could feel wet mush against his fingers as pain lacerated his arm and right shoulder. He was stung with fright and sweat, the torrent of callow brawling.

Curly was furious and stamped forward. He was ignoring the blows that Moses had caught him with. He was rough and strong, even smirking as he came on, his head insensible with blood and mucous. His eyes flared with retaliation as he swarmed into Moses. He flung his arms wide, seeking the slim body of his foe, to draw him into his own sour clinch of immature muscle. Moses flatfooted two, then three steps backwards. He waited until Curly rushed, then with both fists, swung hard. He almost lost his footing and crashed against the decaying clapboards of the saloon. He yelled out at Curly, caught him on the back of the head behind his ear, and Curly reeled from the glancing impact. But it wasn't enough to put him down. He squeezed his eyes then bluffed left to swing a hard loop with his right arm.

Moses was surprised, and hoped to ride the headstrong blow. He took a lot of the pain on his forearm, but the fist smashed sharp and severe into his ribs. He blinked several times as the shock wave pulsed across his chest, and he shook his head in an effort to fling the stinging water from his eyes. Curly's face quivered close to him as he attempted to focus. He wanted something to strike back at, but he just gaped in astonishment and fear. He clawed at his face in the sureness that Curly wasn't going to be satisfied now until he'd destroyed something. It was only for a second or two, but in the distraction another cruel blow smacked into his forehead. It sent him toppling down hard and flat on his shoulder blades. He drew his knees in close, and rolled through the ooze as Curly came leaping in. He was cursing and stomping with a boot heel, hoping to thrust the rasping wedge somewhere in Moses' face. The kick grated across his scalp, and again Curly stumbled.

There was a throbbing roar in Moses' ears that muffled the reality and the distraught shrieks of Erma. He knew he had to get to his feet and fight on. He was dully aware of the tremor of his heart as it pumped away inside him. He had the sensation of ghosts, provoking and dancing luridly in front of him, and didn't understand the illusion. He pushed himself to his feet, and waited as Curly moved towards him. Curly was crazy, and manic coming in again, and Moses stood his ground watching the reckless bending swing of his fist. It was easy to dodge, and Moses stepped inside, making a hard stab into the knotted flesh of Curly's neck. Curly gasped for breath, and threw out his arms wildly. He locked his fingers around Moses' back, clutching them tight against his spine. He pressed with all his remaining strength, and for the first time, Moses glimpsed failure and a beating. The pressure got worse, and Curly crushed the peppery sweat of his body into his face. Moses felt himself being lifted off his feet, and he struggled madly to keep down, and his heels on the ground. His arms and legs were losing their control, and his breath turned shallow, as numbness and dark began to close in. He was twisting his head away from the ugly closeness of the friend who had turned against him. As Moses wearied himself into submission, Curly mistook the effect of his grip and relaxed his hold slightly. It was momentary, but long enough for Moses to respond and wrench his arms free. Without pausing he threw his hands under Curly's jaw and jerked upwards. Curly immediately tried to tighten his arms but Moses had the stand advantage. He straightened his hand and snapped his knuckles into the point of Curly's Adam's apple. The boy instantly fell away, fractured with soundless agony as he clutched at his throat. He sat with his backside in the filthy sodden ground, his body almost crooked double, and he was making odd retching noises in his head. Moses waited for him with an artless mix of insolence and pride, for he sensed, rather than saw there was someone in the back doorway of the saloon, watching. His young temper was burning, and he trembled with emotion.

When Curly staggered to his feet, Moses saw the unbowed look in his eyes and he shuffled in wariness. But Curly's face was contorted and vengeful. It was scratched across the raw bloody features that Moses had made.

Moses stepped back, thinking he had beaten Curly, but, as he retreated from the fight, he glimpsed a dull sparkle of steel. It glanced off the stumpy knife that Curly had drawn from the top of his boot. The craze had returned to his eyes again, swollen and hunted in the shade of the ratrun.

Curly was loudly sucking air as he shambled around Moses. His arms were spread, and they weaved slowly, cobra-like, trying to catch Moses' eye. Very cautiously Moses slid his feet through the spongy filth. He remembered some hand-to-hand combat learning, and kept his eyes fixed on Curly, not on the weapon. Curly's eyes flicked to the right and Moses saw the look. But it wasn't the same as the learning and he understood a fraction too late.

As he spun away, Curly kicked out, and his foot caught Moses behind the right knee sending him sprawling forward. He spread eagled and landed with his face shoved into a mushy run. He caught the thick buzzing of the mosquitoes and fat sawflies. He could see them spinning erratically, and felt them tap his skin as he retched and drew back from the ground.

He heard Curly moving towards him, his feet slurping in the dampness. He somehow knew the knife was on its way, understood the silence of the whirled movement of Curly's arm. He forced himself to move as the blade struck the ground alongside his hand, almost burying itself in the black mud.

Curly grabbed at the top of the haft in an attempt to lever it out, while Moses twisted onto his back, and kicked out with his feet. There was a streak of sunlight directly overhead, and it caught him in the eyes. He saw Curly's figure, vague and blurred, but the blow connected, his heels driving hard into the bone of kneecaps. The impact felled Curly like a woodsman's axe, and he fell with an arm stretched across Moses' waist. Before he could recover, Moses bounded to his feet. Almost in panic he smashed his bunched fist down at the arch of Curly's neck. He uttered a piercing cry of exploit and coup, then trailed Curly as he lumbered away on all fours, driving short chopping blows into the boy's heavy shoulders.

Curly tried to draw his knees up, but failed and collapsed into the mire as another blow took him full and low in the back. He rolled from side to side, trying to extricate himself, spitting blood and slime from his smashed mouth as Moses stood over him. He ranted bloodthirsty oaths and hexes, but had no shrewd or rational response.

He managed to unwind into a crouch, his face and hair smeared thick, black and glutinous. He swayed and trod himself into a tight circle while Moses took his time. The young half-breed mouthed a final charm then lashed out with his foot, a childish but necessary and final marker. Curly headed for a wallow in the vomit and the whiskey piss. It was twilight time, and the day was already over for him.

Moses stood upright and pitched a small toeful of slime across the mildewed shakes of the saloon. It splattered alongside the narrow open doorway, where, for a few moments Erma had stood watching.

Although Moses was trembling, he wasn't troubled by what he'd done, but his adolescent spirit was touched by confusion and sudden, unexpected loneliness. He would run to the river and let the water flow at the dirt and some of the bruises. It was another tough and inescapable rite of passage. But there was a tear of dilemma: he'd been afraid to hit the spike of bone in Curly's back.

* * *

In the alleyway Curly was on his knees, spluttering and feeling his bloody mouth. He looked up, battered and ashamed as Erma stepped down from the saloon. She'd been frightened by the intensity of the boys' fight and didn't want to parcel up any blame. She could see the pain and confusion, and tried to conceal the emotion she felt. 'You're a mess, Curly, but it'll mend. You shouldn't have called him a 'breed. It's the real things that hurt. You of all people should know that.'

Curly snuffled from between his fingers. 'I know.'

'Well, that's the best that could come out of it. If I had a dollar for each time I'd called somebody somethin' I shouldn't, I'd be livin' in clover. So, get yourself cleaned up, an' there's no need for anyone else to know about it. Moses won't mention it, an' I didn't see anythin'.'

Curly was staring at the mess on his hands. 'I don't always get things wrong.'

Erma smiled as she turned away. 'No, Curly, not always. Moses really has to learn how to play cards. You an' me got to learn him.'

Through his blood-congested nose, Curly caught the odour of the filth he was covered in. It suited the way he was feeling, but he was already shaking himself into a better frame of mind. 'Yeeeah, I'll learn him,' he said, but Erma had stepped back inside the saloon.

14

The ticking clock chimed twice for the half-hour, and Ben looked up to see it was 5.30. In less than two hours, the setting sun would be full dropped beyond the western peaks of the Ozarks. It would be sudden, with no pitch to separate dusk from nightfall.

Ben nodded towards the barkeep, placed his only coins on the counter and without hesitation, went out to the street. The stallion threw its nose into the air and stamped a hoof with anticipation. Ben held up the palm of his hand and told it to be quiet. 'There's nothin' to get snorty about. Not yet, anyways.'

Ben's blood cooled when, under the light from a string of happy jack lanterns in the livery barn, he saw two ex-cavalry horses snatching at a hay pile. He saw the blacksmith, and walked towards him, noting the worn leather pouches slung across the horses' withers. The blacksmith was whittling and, as Ben approached, he gave a slight look of annoyance at being disturbed. Ben was bereft of any nicety, and stepped up quickly beside the man's chair. He grabbed at a heavy wool vest, and dragged the surprised man to his feet.

'I don't aim to disturb you for long, feller. I'm lookin' for two or three men, possibly more. About ten years back, they were Fort Denton soldiers. But they still ride together. There's a captain that heads 'em up, an' a lieutenant. They come into town, I want to know *when*.'

The blacksmith stared at him truculently, but didn't reply.

Ben could see the fear, the man's eyes that flicked to the shotgun resting against an animal cage. 'An' where do they go? Them's two real simple questions, feller,' he said.

'They'll kill me if they find out. They

do, if anyone talks.'

Ben methodically pulled his old Navy Colt from around his waist. He ran the barrel around the base of the man's jaw, gave a thin, humourless smile. 'You'll already be dead. I'm puttin' a bullet through your skull right now, if you don't tell me,' he warned. 'You've got two o' their horses right here.'

'They're at the end o' town in the hotel. That's where they are most nights. Pelt an' Ketchum ain't there though. McKay's still scoutin' . . . don't see him much.'

'What do they look like?'

'You'll recognize 'em. They're still wearin' army hats an' breeches. They been runnin' the town for about ten year . . . since they were discharged from Denton. They're guerrillas.'

Ben's manner was emotionless. 'I know what they are.' He released his hold and stepped back a pace. 'You'd be real smart to just finish your whittlin'. Make it a lucky charm,' he advised.

The blacksmith dropped back into his chair. 'I weren't thinkin' o' goin' anywhere.'

Ben tucked the Colt back into his jacket, re-adjusted the pouch across his shoulder and turned into the street. For a moment he stood absolutely still, looked about him for focus and mood. Then he walked along the shallow boardwalk, ran a hand around the stallion's nose as he passed the saloon. 'We're leavin' soon. Probably be after the shootin'.'

He watched both sides of the street and, as he approached the hotel, he heard a harsh shout, then staccato music from a piano. If any of the men he sought were in there, there was a chance they'd have backing. It was an unnecessary risk to go in.

He sat in a deck-chair across the street. The minutes ticked away, and he felt the undercurrents of tension as the sparse community moved unsurely around him. Two cowmen appeared from a narrow alleyway, saddled up and rode to the opposite end of town. Ben sat quietly, sensing the harnessed anger growing inside him. He stood up, trying to control the intense urge to take on the men he felt were inside the hotel. Painfully, he fought against his memories, then stood with his back to the rickety clapboards.

Ten minutes later, and silhouetted against the yellow glow of light from the opening hotel door, he saw two of the men he wanted. They wore faded troopers' uniforms, and, as they stepped down into the street, their faces were partly shadowed by battered hats. They carried army issue Colts, holstered high around their waists, and one of them had the ragged stripes of a corporal hanging from his arm. Ben could make out the glint from metal tunic buttons, the military embellishments sharpening his grief. For a moment the two men stood talking, and they didn't notice Ben moving from the darkness across the street until he was less than a dozen feet away.

'You two,' he said, his words flat, but effecting, 'I been waitin' to ask you somethin'.'

The troopers looked at each other and shrugged. Then with little concern they turned back to Ben. 'Make it quick,' one of them said.

'Think back ten years, to Horse Creek Lakes. Was it you attacked an' killed a small band o' Cheyenne? Women an' children' Cheyenne.'

The corporal man answered, careless and indifferent. 'Well, that is a time ago. We killed a lot in them days. Can't rightly separate it all out.' The man was wary and he peered forward into the darkness. His practised cunning sensed danger, and he moved sideways away from his colleague, ready to outflank Ben. 'You carryin' a problem? Who the hell's askin'?' he demanded.

'*I* don't matter, but my family did. You're the scum that murdered 'em, an' you never got punished.'

The corporal glanced indolently up and down the dark street. 'Injun lovers should get 'emselves up to the Nations. There's still plenty red meat there, if you're wantin' to restock.'

Ben groaned inwardly and his gut hardened. He felt the empty coldness that he'd lived with for all those years. He unwound the rawhide sash from his neck and held the Navy Colt at his side. He waited for a sign of movement, but it wasn't possible to keep his eyes on both of them; that's what they were relying on. There was a boorish sneer from the corporal on the left, but Ben didn't flinch. He knew then that it would be him who'd shoot first.

A stream of light suddenly cut between them as the door of the hotel opened again, and a drunk staggered out. Ben knew it was the moment, and he saw the corporal grab for his gun.

Before the long barrel had cleared the corporal's holster, Ben's wrist was bucking, as he thumbed back the hammer of his Colt. The guerrilla soldier jerked back as the bullet struck him in the chest. He was lifted up on his toes, as if trying to appear bigger, then he pitched forward, slamming into the hard-packed dirt of the street. Ben watched as the man's gun hand dragged at his Colt, but it was too late and the body finally caved in. Ben stepped forward and toe-rolled the lifeless ex-army corporal. He looked at the dead face, then back at the second man. 'I guess his answer was, yes,' he grated.

The trooper stood rooted to the spot. He gaped with foreboding at Ben. 'I ain't army, mister . . . never was. Like to wear the uniform . . . mix with 'em, that's all,' he lied. 'That other stuff was o' no matter to me. I want out o'here.'

Ben pulled back the hammer for the second time, shook his head. 'Well, you're goin' feller,' he said with lethal certainty.

The trooper had to make a try to live, and he made a futile grab for his Colt. Ben waited for him to level the gun, and he hissed through his teeth as the doomed man palmed the hammer with his other hand. Ben's bullet caught him in the left shoulder, spinning him round with the impact. Clutching his gun in both hands, the trooper managed to fire one shot that ploughed into the ground between his buckling legs. Ben fired again, and the man crashed back against the wooden railing that fronted the board-walk. He hung there for several seconds, then fell, throwing his gun out ahead of him.

Ben looped the sash back around his neck, and tucked the Colt under his tattered skin coat. There was movement on the sidewalk, in the shadows several people gathered to look down at the two bodies. No one seemed to particularly care about doing anything. Ben looked around the faces as if encouraging a reprisal, then he moved off. Walking unhurriedly across the street, he stood in an alley and gave one, short piercing whistle.

★ ★ ★

Moses was back in the River Bend. He was disturbed and breathless, spoke quickly as he sat down.

'Who was he?' he asked, looking closely at Erma. 'I saw him . . . heard him say there was an Indian killing, ten years ago at Horse Creek Lakes. He said it's where his family was murdered by the army. They were Cheyenne, Erma. You know who he is?'

Erma looked into Moses' blue eyes. 'I'm not sure. But I saw him too, Moses. If it is him . . . who I think it is, he'll be back. He's not yet finished with the soldiers.'

Moses got up from the table and walked frustratedly around the bar room. He went over to the door and looked out, up and down the street. He turned round, stared at Erma, and came back slowly towards her. He'd calmed himself, and stood very still and contained. 'He was the man who stood at the bar earlier . . . who ate half an egg. There were signs on his coat. If he comes back, I'll know.'

Erma continued looking at Moses, then she touched the back of his hand.

'I know you will, Moses,' she said. 'An' that's *when* he comes back, not *if*. Why don't you go an' see if Curly's OK?' she added, not entirely as an afterthought.

15

Ben rode out fast, back towards the foothills. The land threw crimson light into his face, but the scrub and distant Ozarks stood darkly silhouetted against the disappearing sun. The stream that had earlier led them towards Lizard Wells, now sparkled gold as it wove its way across the flat, crumpled land. They galloped straight and at speed until they met the breezes that drifted down from the distant snowline. Then they slowed to a canter, until the last of the day's light slipped away. They stopped and listened to the sounds of their own heavy breathing, and finches roosting in the scrub. Ben dismounted and let the reins drop from his fingers. He walked ahead into the blue night, and felt the warmth of his stallion's nose loyally rubbing the small of his back.

His retribution on those responsible for the murder of his family had begun. His hands dropped to his sides, and as he faced the high range, the words of a Cheyenne song came to him.

> . . . *there was no rain and no corn*
> *so they moved at last,*
> *Hanan ey yaa ney haa*
> *To food and shelter and a pleas-*
> *ant plain,*
> *Nanan ey yaa Hanan ey yaa . . .*

'Goddamn Cheyenne had a goddamn song for everythin'," he muttered with affecting irony.

★ ★ ★

When early morning shards of grey and pink eased their way across the vast Missouri sky, Ben was lying full length in one of the fast, shallow waters of the Piney. He was fully dressed with his chin in his hands resting on a smooth round boulder. He could just hear the singing of the gnats as they raced above the swirling eddies, and under his nose a tiny water spider sculled a route across the mighty rapids of his clasped fingers. He had enough remaining provisions for him and his horse to eat and drink. Their predicament wasn't entirely planned, but he reckoned it was a tad safer than a hotel room back in Lizard Wells.

The previous evening they'd made twenty to twenty-five miles, and long before midnight, he'd cooked up a mash of chopped apple and clover honey. He'd feasted off bacon and cornmeal fritters.

He rolled over onto his back with his head downstream, felt the cold water embrace his thickening beard. He lay there for many minutes, oblivious to the sounds of silence in the outside world. But eventually the clean sharp chill started to find its way inside him and he shivered extravagantly. He put two fingers to his mouth and gave a short piercing whistle. He would let the stallion drag him up and onto the low, sloping bank.

He waited for a few moments, and rolled back onto his front. He couldn't see his horse, and he raised himself onto his elbows. He scanned the area of near bank and across the small campsite. There was no sign of the stallion, and he stumbled quickly to his knees, slipping and sliding on the stony river bed. He sloshed through the shallows to the bank and searched the flat scrubland.

★　★　★

There were three of them, and they never came closer than half a mile during the early morning dark. Ben had heard nothing, and even if he had, from that distance they could have shot him as he clambered from the stream, before he got to his guns. He could see them plainly, colourless but definite against the low sun. They'd brought an oestrus mare, and stood off, using the only enticement his ground-hitched stallion would respond to.

It would have caught an enchanting drift on the light westerly breeze, and from that distance would have wandered off on an interested walk. But within 200 yards the stallion would have a clear sighting, and its senses would be fully aroused. There was no faith or whistling potent enough to compete with that prime instinct, and the chances of him returning to Ben during that journey were remote.

They rode away in single-file, with the mare and stallion in the rear. Leading at a trot was McKay, the scout. The guerrilla army leader, Captain Gideon Pelt and his lieutenant, Farr Ketchum, were trailing in line with a lead on the horses.

With the Springfield, Ben could have dropped all three, but they had considered that, and presented him with a narrow target protected by his precious stallion.

He watched them for nearly an hou

until the early heat-shimmer rose to envelop them. Then all that remained was a few darkish specks sinking in a surface of rippling shadows.

They'd found out about him from the blacksmith. They came specifically for his horse, wanting to draw him back to Lizard Wells, or to die in the attempt. Either way, it was for their mean and wanton entertainment.

In a straight line, the town was more than twenty miles, but following the contours of the stream, nearer fifty. By day and on foot, the surface would be a murderous searing hot-plate. It was unthinkable, unless he did follow the stream, and that would take three or four days. Night travel would take even longer, with its own primitive fears. Ben had no choice: he had to make the journey with his guns, waterskin, canvas saddle pouch and a well-honed capacity for endurance.

He drew his Springfield from its ¹ and levered out the breech-
ᵒ ᵗhout taking his eyes off the

horizon he pressed one round into the firing chamber and pulled on the trigger guard. He rested the stock against his hip, cocked the hammer and squeezed the trigger. The crack of the single shot would carry a vast distance, and within a few seconds reach the minds and ears of the riders ahead. It was Ben's salute to their venture and guile. But it was also a stark warning of his intention to survive and return.

16

On the outskirts of Lizard Wells, Moses laid across the cool flats watching the surface of the river as it swerved towards him. He dipped his foot into the purling water and trapped a fragment of dark fur across the toe of his shabby moccasin. It was nothing more than a sodden, tangled shred, but it still held a sinew stitch and the shard of a bear claw.

He slid into the water and crawled through a shoal of reflections until he reached the far bank of the Piney. He stood with his back to the town and looked west towards the distant silhouette of the Ozarks.

An emotion corded inside him, and he closed his eyes and sucked air noisily ugh his teeth. There was something an unapproachable memory scrap he held tight within

McKay removed the rope halter from the Appaloosa stallion's neck. Using the oestrus mare, he'd coaxed him into one of the cracked barns that edged the town. It was going to be a test, the sort of encounter that revealed the cruel slant of the one-time army scout. In a corral, at the open end of the barn, a uniformed colleague held in a dun-coloured mustang. It was untried, and still wild after six weeks of torment in confined squalor.

Ben's big Appaloosa saw the wild horse immediately, and in his uncertainty and unfamiliar surroundings, rubbed in close to the logged bars of the corral. He turned his head from sideways on, alarmed and defensive. The dun snorted aggressively, and stamped towards the inevitable attack. It came on, but the Appaloosa didn't shy away. Instead he moved forward, his steps light and cautious.

The stallions swung their faces in

141

close, overlapping until their jowls were almost touching. Deliberately the dun lowered its great bony head. It was a slow movement, dire and threatening, but the Appaloosa didn't argue with the challenge. The stallions wove powerful arcs with their necks, cutting and thrusting, until the head of each horse was probing between the forefeet of his opponent. They were set in their efforts to get lower, and they pressed until their blazing nostrils were within a few inches of the ground.

They sucked in great draughts of air until their necks were corded and swollen. Their chests bulged with anticipation, and for a while they remained still, their muscles tightly sprung and shimmering in the flat evening dark. It was the silence of impending combat, and nothing moved, only their fleshy nostrils that blew violent squalls of dust across the pummelled ground. Each horse was seeking leverage and supremacy, sensing and waiting for a sign of weakness. It ended suddenly when the dun squealed and whirled in a complete circle, twisting its hindquarter and lashing out with its massive hoofs.

The preliminaries were over, and from fifteen feet the dun rose on its cannons and advanced like a fist-fighter intending to smash its way ahead. Its flailing forelegs pounded the air head on to the Appaloosa, but the stallion railed from the bone-crushing attack and swung round to thrash his own rear hoofs low at the enraged mustang. There was one glancing strike, but it caught the dun in the ribs and drew a sharp bellow. It dropped to all fours and whirled to face the Appaloosa. There was a shuddering rage in its scream, and it sprayed fountains of saliva high across the pen. The Appaloosa was driving it to more frustration, and the dun pounded the ground in fury.

With its jaws spread, and the cutting edges of its great molars bared, the dun rushed, but the Appaloosa wasn't there. He'd leaped from the punishing teeth that could snap a leg bone as if it was a bar of candy. He'd moved out of range, tempting and very dangerous. The dun's rage carried it into one angry bellowing charge after another, its shoulders heaving and sweat darkening its jugular run.

The Appaloosa was presenting one opportunity after another, but was evading each attack by muscle and swerve, driving the big dun into a fury of bewilderment and disorientation. There was an inevitable open moment when it lagged in turning round, and both of the Appaloosa's hind feet landed solidly against its ribs. The dun grunted with pain, and its great strength suddenly faltered and showed signs of uncertainty. It came to a halt, and stood in the centre of the pen glaring belligerently at its elusive opponent. Its flanks were heaving from the exertion, and rivers of sweat were dripping from its belly.

The Appaloosa sensed victory and pranced tantalizingly close. There was no response from the dun, and it veered from the onslaught. It tried to move away, but the Appaloosa swung around in front barring its progress, edging a half-step forward, springing his heels in a sharp gesture.

★　★　★

From his watching station along the Piney, Moses heard the murderous whinnies piercing the night air. His skin tingled, and he sprang from the shallows. He understood the noise and ran swiftly and unseen to the corrals. He slithered under the raised floor of a cabin, and brought himself to the outer poles of the corral. He immediately recognized the horse. It belonged to the man who'd shot the soldiers, the man who'd had an Indian wife, who'd told of his family. The sight, within thirty feet of him, was startling and terrifying.

★　★　★

Both stallions stood very still, their bodies merging into the dusk. They flexed and panted, darkly silhouetted against the pen rails and the flats beyond. A few seconds passed while they measured each other for gesture and nerve, then the Appaloosa whirled and flew into another attack. The dun was surprised by the quickness of the move, and then the Appaloosa was above it, towering on his hind legs and driving with punching forefeet. The dun started in retreat, backing away confusedly, but not before a cruel blow slashed into one of its ears. The Appaloosa chased his advantage, balancing on his hind feet, using his fore hoofs like fists. The dun emitted an enraged scream and abandoned its attempt to break away. Using brute strength, it came up through the driving whirl of its opponents hoofs, taking blows on its neck and chest to settle a face-off with the Appaloosa.

The dun was half blinded by the blood that cascaded across the side of its head from the torn ear, but it seemed oblivious to pain and the blows it was receiving. It struck out with its huge bony hoofs in desperate frenzy, and the Appaloosa threw out his head in an attempt to seize one of the punishing forelegs. But before the Appaloosa realized it, a powerful gnash raked down his neck and ripped out a great wad of hair and outer hide.

The Appaloosa went down on his knees, but kept his balance. He thrust himself up, and in the same instant caught the dun squarely on the chest with his driving hind feet. The dun retaliated with another seizure from its jaws. It opened two deep gashes in the Appaloosa's hip, and blood welled across the sweat-stained buttock.

★ ★ ★

Across the corral, Moses could see that McKay had been joined by three or four other men. They were laughing and joshing, and Moses caught some of their words above the fearful noise.

'No one's goin' to ride him after this.

He's goin' back to the wild. Ten dollars says he'll kill the dun.'

In the fading light, Moses saw then tossing coins and folding money at each others feet. He realized they were making wagers on the outcome of the fight, and he wanted the man to come back as Erma said he would.

* * *

The dun came to a halt on spraddled legs and stood there, exhausted and blinded. Sweat dripped from its body, and blood trickled in thin streams across its muzzle. Dimly it saw the Appaloosa coming back to the attack, and gamely it reared and struck. But its feet found only thin air. A succession of blows was rained against its right shoulder, thudding in a blanket of foaming sweat. The blows then came from the left side, landing high on its withers. It threw its weight into the Appaloosa, seeking to knock him down, but the stallion whirled and landed on all fours. He lashed out his hind feet, and one of them caught the dun on the lower jaw. The great hoof pounded through soft flesh, and crushed teeth and bone. The dun turned, reared once and charged. It took great strides, thrusting madly at the air, hooking and scything with its front hoofs, but the Appaloosa skidded away. The dun dropped back to earth and turned to face its adversary, but its movements were exhausted and clumsy.

* * *

McKay and the men with him grabbed at the money in front of them. They made vehement noises and moved off in the direction of the hotel. Moses watched unnerved and angry as they pushed and shoved each other, kicking and spitting at the ground. He pulled himself on to his elbows, dragged himself to a broken water trough that abutted the corral, and flung his senses back to the horses.

The mustang was beaten and knew it. Its strength was gone, and the power and quickness had flown from its legs. There was no escape, and it stood and defended itself as best it could. It tried to locate its adversary through the bloody mist, dodging and parrying, occasionally giving ground, but still dogged and reluctant. The Appaloosa returned to the attack, lashing without mercy. Drenched with blood and sweat, he went about the task of beating his opponent to the earth. But the dun was hard, and took the blows, even after it had even ceased to defend. It was a mass of bruises, of cuts and gashes, and its jaw hung cruel and broken. It stood with its four legs spread, and braced itself, anger and defiance still in its heart. But at last as the night descended, its big bony knees buckled and it slid slowly to the damp scarred earth. The mustang turned on its side and crooked its neck, a great sigh came heavy and full-flecked from its nostrils.

The Appaloosa raised his head which gleamed hard and lustrous in the first dark.

Moses was awe-struck. The air was oppressive and filled with raw sensations. His heart was pounding and it hurt, and he buried his face in the crook of his arm.

17

At her usual table in the River Bend Saloon, Erma Flagg was sipping her whiskey. She was in a poker game with Moses and an off-course trooper of the guerrilla army. Moses was unhappy, searching through his fist of cards. He had a bottle of beer in front of him and a thumb-sized cork in a corner of his mouth. Youngsters didn't grow up in towns like Lizard Wells, there was never a chance; they hauled their way up to the first set of double figures, then leapt headlong into whatever remained.

Moses had been watching the man, Coney Rimmer. He'd been taking from Erma, and Moses knew he'd been cheating. The underlings of Captain Pelt's company thought it their right. He made an almost imperceptible nod at Erma and moved noiselessly away from the table. He stayed away five minutes, relieving himself in the adjoining alley.

Rimmer slammed his 'trick' face down onto the table. The drinking glasses rattled and Rimmer grasped the bottle of sour whiskey. He glanced rudely at Erma. 'Is that 'breed kid ever comin' back? He must've seen my threes. My first winnin' hand o' the day.' He wiped his mouth and nose simultaneously across the sleeve of his ragged tunic, oblivious to the scab of slime that stretched from wrist to elbow.

Moses walked slow and resolute back to the table. He looked regretfully at Erma, then turned his gaze on Rimmer. It wasn't the card cheating, it was that Moses suddenly recognized him as one of the men he'd seen betting and jeering cruelly as the stallions had fought, two hours before. Moses was burned up, and he nodded provokingly at the clutch of the man's hand. 'One of those cards came from your sleeve, not the pack.'

The trooper leaned forward and ran his fingers around the inside of his boot. He straightened his back and lifted his arm quickly, but it wasn't fast enough for Moses to miss. He drove his fingers in hard against the man's neck, watching the face as it twisted down into the card table. There was a clatter on the floor, and Moses bent down and picked up a thin-bladed knife. He flicked it on the table and pulled at the guerrilla soldier. The man had split his lips and, from his open mouth, blood welled across his big yellowing front teeth.

Moses could see by the look on Erma's face there was something wrong, and he turned to see two more troopers advancing towards him. One of them held out a broken sabre, its snapped point waving at his chest. The man tut-tutted, shook his head and turned to his colleague. 'We got us a young 'breed, if I ain't mistaken. A 'breed that's gone an' done somethin' real bad . . . a skinnin' offence, if ever I seen one. Why don't we make him a full-blood?'

Moses was aware of his standing in Lizard Wells, and the need to keep away from trouble that flowed with the guerrilla company. He swept the glasses, cards, whiskey bottle and lighted candle from the table. In the instant the troopers ducked and swung away, he was off. He sprang across a table near the door and flung himself into the street. Within minutes he'd disappeared among the shanties and flop tents at the southern end of town. Even the hard-bitten were reluctant to follow into that den of pollution and depravity.

The troopers took a long hard look at Erma, then grabbed at the card cheat. By the way they dragged him across the floor, Erma was certain that Moses had hit him with a fatal blow. She snarled at them as they pulled the body through the door.

'Tell your captain he had a knife in his boot, an' a card up his sleeve.'

After listening to Erma, Sheriff

Derby Crewes decided to let the matter rest. He'd known Erma for many years, and although he was deferential to the army men, he believed her story. Furthermore, Moses was too young to warrant a hard sentence, and Gideon Pelt usually took care of his own law enforcement. 'Get him to lie low, Erma. Use them Indian skills o' his,' he said.

Thoughtfully, Erma left the sheriff's office. She was troubled, deeply concerned. Had Moses started on his warpath of retribution for the slaughter of his mother at Horse Creek Lakes, ten years ago? At such an early age, had he sought the opportunity to make his first soldier killing? Was he unknowingly running with his father, Ben Brooke?

18

Ben faced the shimmering horizon. He sensed the route of a probable course back to Lizard Wells, and with his remaining grips he took a determined south of east trail into nowhere.

For five hours he walked under the blazing sun. His feet, and the top of his head were scorched through the beaten crown of his hat. No longer was there any shelter, not the slightest wedge of shade or hollow scrape. He gripped his bone-handled knife and smoothed his fingers across the carved relief. He felt the hard edge of the blade, and remembered the small Cheyenne band of the northern territories.

An image of Blue Sky blistered itself into his mind as he staggered on. He pulled the knife from his pocket, but he couldn't see the carving in the bleached bone of the handle. His eyes were stinging, his senses were scrambled by the blinding light that beat up from the desert floor. He turned the small knife in his hand, but his fingers slipped, and he almost dropped it. He heard sounds like water, but it was only the soft swish of the thin, desert sand as he stumbled forward. His body was burning up, and he ripped at the remains of his coat, tearing it away from his chest until it hung in rags around his waist. He thought of the soldiers who had murdered his wife and child. No longer could he separate reality from the shifting mirages, and he slipped into the land of anguish and visions.

* * *

His dog was far ahead when it sniffed water, but it was a stagnant pool lying in some higher ground. The buffaloes had been wallowing in the stinking liquid, but Bull was raving with thirst, and plunged his nose to lap and suck at the diseased water. It was the recklessness of finding, and he drank to excess. From twenty paces, Ben watched helplessly as the animal's neck muscles lost control and its head began to fall. He stumbled forward to the edge of the mire and, as his legs buckled, Bull swayed softly against his legs. It yipped once and collapsed across Ben's bloodied feet. He kneeled painfully to scratch the tight, matted hair above the dog's dark muzzle, and he made soothing noises as he watched Bull's stomach heave with the bilious soup.

The heat was so intense it was thickening the pool. The overpowering stench of rotting algae was liquefying the roof of Ben's mouth. He stared dully into Bull's eyes. He pressed his chafed hands into the short, warm hair, gently kneaded the collapsed sinews.

Bull was the young bulldog that had fought the Malamute in the fighting pit outside of the walls of Fort Denton. Ben had rescued the dog, taken it to hunt bear and beaver in the timberline above Horse Creek Lakes, the plentiful hunting grounds once so beloved of a small band of Cheyenne.

Ben tried to focus on the sleeping form of Bull, but the shimmering ribbons of heat wound with salt water and filled his eyes. His body convulsed and a tormenting choke clawed its way from deep and concealed within him. His head fell forward and he curved tortuously to the ground, crushing life from the quietness and suffering of his dog. Ben pulled his face away from the ground. He dragged thin rasping spasms from lungs that were hot and charred with dust.

★　★　★

But there was no dog or stagnant pool. Ben looked at his hands. They were finely etched with skeins of blood, brown and congealed in the creases of his scorched skin. He moved his fingers across the bridge of his nose, wincing at the sharp cut of pain from something broken. His feet were swollen, blistered and clawed from the vicious mesquite. He rolled onto his side, and then onto his back and the slanting sun detonated the centre of his forehead.

There hadn't been any Bull on the lifeless plain. He'd died more than two years ago; had suffered a heart attack after the excitement of chasing a racoon up a tree. It was the start of the trial, and a warning to Ben's instinct for staying alive. The dream was over, but the nightmare of reality was a rat-fly drilling for sustenance between the splinter of his toes.

During the countless hours of his nightmare, Ben had travelled far from the Piney. He scrambled up, and with approaching panic scanned the near ground. There was no sign of his water-skin or his hat. But his Springfield and saddle pouch were within a few paces. His Navy Colt was in the pouch with his silver and a small amount of ammunition.

He peeled off the remains of his sweat-encrusted coat and placed it on the ground beneath his foot. He stretched futilely against the sinew stitches until he remembered his knife. He sliced the tough threads around one of the sleeves and pulled the piece of doeskin over the top of his head. It was rapidly approaching midday, and the sun was arching up to its unique killing zone. He lost track of time. For hours, the land had opened and closed its great jaws from shimmering light to blackness. He tripped and stumbled until finally his legs buckled him into the debris of bleached bone and petrified mesquite.

⋆ ⋆ ⋆

Evening and night had passed, twelve hours since Ben had collapsed into the arid plain. He felt the chill drawing at his back, but the first rolls of daylight were already playing across his face. He turned his head sharply and raised a cloud of fine salty dust. It strangled his nose and throat, and he coughed and sneezed. The agitation wrenched some life into him, and he strained to see the land for markers or standpoint.

It was too much and too early, and he lay for another hour as the last stars faded from the sky. The dawn slowly withered, and he eased himself onto his knees and peered towards Horse Creek Lakes.

The air became warmer and the sky was turning light blue and free from cloud. The long spare shadows of the early hours withdrew across the land, and the sun broke from a shoulder of the distant mountain range. He shielded his eyes with his hand and turned to the west, judging the caustic barrenness. Everything was blurred, and he savagely contemplated the distance from Lizard Wells.

He clenched his fists and looked down at Blue Sky's trimmings — the knots of beaver fur and bear claws she'd woven into the remnants of his coat. The heat rose from his body and he scented the unmistakable pungency of tribal odour. It encouraged the feral lure for survival, and without affliction or deceit he sought the help of Tirawa, the legendary 'father' of the Cheyenne and Pawnee:

Hear my voice ye warlike birds,
like you I shall go.
I wish the swiftness ofyour wings,
I wish the vengeance ofyour claws,
I follow your flight,
Look with wrath on the battlefield.

'Yeah, a goddamn song for everythin',' he spluttered. Close by, a small desert cricket flicked its feet. In seconds it buried itself in the sand, seeking shelter from the impending heat of the day.

During the night it managed to collect moisture from the nearby shallows of the Piney, but Ben hadn't heard or seen it. It was an odd crispness of air and soft liquid murmuring that alerted him to the closeness of water.

His address to Tirawa and the spirits

164

of eagles were a form of thanks and guidance. But for so many hours, his painful, insect-bitten foot had slanted him into the trail of a ten-mile circle. Lizard Wells was still twenty miles in a straight line, fifty by the contours of the stream.

★   ★   ★

It was early evening in Lizard Wells. In the saloon, the usual few diehard customers sat around with their whiskey and cards. Erma sat talking with Osuno and Moses. Since his fight with the soldier, Moses had become uneasy and remote. He'd spent less time in town, and with Osuno's trips out to the timberline, Erma was feeling another creep of loneliness. They were waiting for something to happen, something in which they were all included. They were waiting-out, because none of them knew the closeness of a natural family.

Moses was drumming his fingers on the table. From the time Ben Brooke had gunned down the two guerrilla soldiers outside the hotel, Erma knew the question was coming.

Moses' eyes flicked from Osuno to Erma. 'You said, he'll be back. Who is he? You said you know him.'

Erma looked considerately at Moses. 'That ain't quite what I said, Moses, but he *will* be back. He'll come back for his horse. Then he'll take the soldiers, Pelt an' Ketchum . . . McKay too.'

Moses looked thoughtfully at Erma. 'Tell me what you know of him?'

'I think he's your father, Moses. Your mother would've been among them that got massacred by the soldiers. I'm sorry, but I didn't know it until he killed those troopers. That's the long truth of it.'

Moses held out the shard of bear claw, and squeezed it in the palm of his hand. 'He is my father. He'd tribe signs stitched into his coat. He stood over there at the bar; I saw him. When he comes back, I'll help him.'

Osuno placed a strong hand on the

boy's shoulder. 'I can't say you're too young, Moses, an' you know I'm not one for givin' advice, but there's some men as need help, and there's some as don't. I reckon the man who's comin' back here's one o' *them*. I'm goin' back to the timberline for tradin'. I won't be here.'

Osuno had reached the end of his talk. 'He's your pa, Moses. Whatever you decide on, jus' remember your learnin'.'

19

Ben lowered his face into the Piney. He was gripping his painful muscles, and it was a few seconds before he felt the softening effect of the water against his eyes and mouth. His ran his swollen tongue against his teeth and gums. He spat down into the swirl beneath him, closed his mouth and pushed his face once more under the shallow stream. He twisted his neck sideways against the current, feeling the smooth hardness of the pebbles against his ear, and he smelled the clear water as it rolled around the side of his face. He pulled himself upright on the bank, and started to remove the remnants of his filthy clothing.

He crouched naked in the Breaks. The Piney was running through his threadbare johns, and his torn coat and breeches lay drying on the low angled bank. It was nearly mid-morning, and real hunger was beginning to cause him grief. His silver couldn't buy him anything, and there was no chance to shoot animals or birds during the heat of the day.

He looked along the banks of the river for something edible, onions and berries, or rushes and ferns for their roots. He wanted something for the pain in the bones of his head, and it was vital that he found shelter, a bolt-hole from the draw of the sun. Now was the time to make use of those years spent living along the timberline, how to hold-up and survive.

Ben knew the signs, and the most likely places for sustenance. He used the stock of his rifle as a digging stick in the moister ground that fringed the stream. If he could focus his mind, he would gain a meal and then he could forge a route back to Lizard Wells.

As the sun rose higher, he found the wild onions. He started a small fire the Indian way, with dried splints, but improvised with long john fluff and parched bracken. The onions were small but moist, and with licorice fern and a handful of plump crickets, he roasted a meagre but tasty meal.

It was approaching noon, and he wrapped the loops of his saddle pouch around the long barrel of the Springfield. He used the stock as a footing brace and, with the Navy Colt looped to his wrist, he set himself along the stream towards Lizard Wells. He was starting east, but ahead of him the current bent continually in its serpentine drift to the outskirts of town. The current pressed the back of his legs, and the flat stones massaged his feet. The water was crystal clear, and every now and again he caught sight of a scuttling crayfish or a fresh-water clam. He jammed his pouch with half a dozen of each, and draped the sopping canvas across the top of his head.

His appearance was raw and startling, his sinews were either knotted or twisted, and his bones ached. But he was finding his old resilience, and the purpose for his return was biting.

It was nearly midday when Ben found what he was looking for. It was a large, flat-topped boulder that shelved into the bank of the stream. There was low shelter beneath it, and from noon it would be refuge from the burning slant of the sun. He eased himself into the narrow cleft and pushed his effects into a close hollow.

He stretched out his arm and ran his fingers around a mud stamp that led from the edge of the stream. It was one of many that curled around the low bank before tracking out onto the plain. The iron shoes had been removed, but Ben knew and responded to the hoof print. It was as moving and unforgettable as it had been when he'd tracked and finally won the Appaloosa. The memories wafted in around him. Then the silence and isolation created the void he needed. Within five minutes he'd drifted into an abyss of sleep.

Ben was aware of the musty animal tang as he woke from his darkness. He stared up into the face of a human buffalo, and instinctively groped behind him for his Colt. But the apparition grunted from deep in his throat, and forced the barrel end of the Springfield down into Ben's shoulder.

'You're in no shape to try that,' the mountain man growled at him. 'If I'd wanted to skin you, I could've done it anytime durin' the night.'

Ben had slept unconscious for eighteen hours. He blinked against the dawning light, and painfully eased himself to his knees. He looked around him, and saw two sway-backed mules standing twenty feet away in the middle of the stream.

'I can only guess at which way you're headed, but the mess you're in, you'll never get there. I was markin' you down for a dead 'un all right.' The man spat a thin stream of dark juice over his shoulder and took a step back. 'Either that or distant kin,' he rumbled, with a short laugh.

Ben climbed stiffly to his feet. 'Where the hell d'you come from?'

The mountain man hawked down into the sand. 'From where there's critters,' he answered. 'I supply 'em to the livery. An' I'm wonderin' what I'd get for you.'

Ben stood unprotected and vulnerable, rubbing his hands together. 'So you're goin' to Lizard Wells?'

'Lizard Wells is where I'm *from*, you dope. Do you see any other critters with me but them mules?'

Ben stared around him at the desolate flats. 'Well, you ain't much use to me then. Just give me my gun back, an' point me in the right direction.'

The mountain man looked Ben up and down. He squinted, his eyes crinkled like walnuts.

'The Wells is a bad place for someone in your condition, mister. Most folk are lookin' like you, when they come away.'

Ben squinted back at him. 'These are

my workin' duds,' he said. 'I got a horse to collect, an' there's some renegade army with a debt needs settlin'. They ain't worth dressin' up for.'

Another deep, chesty laugh broke from the mountain man. 'Well, could be I know what you're meanin', son. The reasonin' won't be my business.'

Ben rubbed the back of his neck and attempted a spit. 'That's right. It's real personal. Has been for nigh on ten years.'

The mountain man yanked at his greasy skin trousers. 'Hmm, ten years, eh?' He looked closely into Ben's eyes. 'Don't let revenge get the drop on you. Take 'em 'cause you *want* to. It jus' might keep you alive.'

Ben turned his head sideways-on to the old trapper. 'It matters to you then, does it?' he asked.

'That's for me to know, son, an' I ain't a man to go explainin'. But you get to live, so maybe you'll find out,' he said. 'An' you'll have need o' this.' The mountain man nodded obligingly, held out Ben's Springfield. 'The ones you want are Captain Gideon Pelt an' his scout, Bolton McKay. Look out for Farr Ketchum, he's Pelt's lieutenant. I know there's two less of 'em, but there'll be more o' course. They're all trash . . . cowardly rabble, an' the very meanest sons o' bitches. Take 'em out early, an' if I got it right, they shouldn't give a man like you too much trouble.' The oldster spat another stream of juice, then walked over to his mules to untie a sack of provisions. 'You ever owned a dog?' he asked, as if a thought had suddenly struck him. 'A mean, black-hearted son-of-a bitch?'

Ben thought for a moment, before giving the old man a questioning look. 'I might've done. Only the dog I had, was the original bitch, an' no one ever *owned* it. Have we met before?' he wanted to know.

'Reckon we might've done,' the mountain man returned enigmatically. 'Oh yeah, that handsome Appaloosa? He's in a corral at the south end o' town,' he added, with a shrewd grin.

20

It was night-time, and Ben was within a quartermile of Lizard Wells. At the start of the day, the mountain man had helped him collect his thoughts and prepare. He'd been able to tend his aches and pains with burdock and willow herb. Ben had even managed to scrape down most of his beard.

Riding one of the mules, it had been a further four-hour journey, but his new resolve and a bellyful of trapper stew and hot coffee had fortified him for the long awaited confrontation. Now Ben *wanted* the men who were responsible for the murder of his family.

He made a cautious advance on the broken ribbons of light, circuiting to the north and lying close to the flat banks of the Piney. He dismounted and pulled down his Springfield and canvas pouch, then he watched the mule turn back to the desert and the mountain man.

The river looped around the small town, as if by will and wisdom keeping its distance. The water was beginning to widen and harvest strength in its journey towards an encounter with the Mississippi, and only in two places did it touch the outskirts.

From the corner of his eye, Ben sensed movement across the flats. It was at the limit of his vision, and he strained to see the form of someone rising slowly to their feet. There was a sureness and strength in the easy movement, and it flicked a page in his memory. He held himself in close to the low rolling bank, and for a few moments watched fascinated as Moses stood in the shallows.

Ben waded the furthest bend of the river, then crawled until he could see the light from oil lamps hung behind dusty windows. From the hotel, he could hear the sounds of the piano struggling with the tune of 'Dancin' Britches'.

He turned to the short furrowed alleys and moved warily until he reached the spine of the main street. He knelt low amongst the garbage of the shanties, listened to the town's visceral night-fall.

A voice reached out from the saloon, and he shrank back as light from its half-open doorway cut a pale yellow shaft down into the street. There was a stocky Mexican hobbling on the ground, wresting the lower half of his long johns with one hand, and waving a battered hat in the other. He was calling mercies, insistently and plaintively to a scantily clad woman. '*Que pasa, Maria . . . que pasa?*' She was wearing loose woolly drawers and jemmy boots.

She called out, '*Bastardo burro,*' and staggered drunkenly towards the livery stable. Against the light of a nearby window, Ben could see two faces peering into the dark. One of them was laughing at the drama, and the other was rapping his knuckles against the smeared, dusty glass. He watched the

Mexican sink to his knees, distraught in lusty confusion.

Further to the west of town, candles guttered in a cabin that leaned against the side of a animal pen. There was a man with his foot on the gate throwing food in the direction of a snuffling hog. He was humming a tune, then singing, and Ben could hear some of the words.

'Don't you see the golden city, and the everlasting day.'

Ben had heard it before. It was a prospectors' song of optimism from somewhere out on the Breaks many years ago. 'All get yourselves ready for some proper entertainment,' he suggested quietly.

A derisive smile had hardly faded when he killed the rat. Presumptuously, it was nosing the sole of his foot, and Ben swore, smashed the oily brown head with the frame of his Colt. He shuddered, then backed off twenty or thirty paces from the side of the street. His stomach had started to churn, and he smelled the town as its whiff scuttled strong and close to the ground. Animal fur, dust, tobacco, stables, wood fire, can-houses, swill. It was all there, rolling towards him like a fermenting carpet.

He turned away in unease, back to the darkness. The moon was early in its first quarter, and the sky was turning from deep grey to black. From the Ozarks, thick clouds had formed and distant thunder rolled out across the Breaks. Within hours rain would slam across the town, and Ben had to make a move. He edged his way south, along the backs of the shanties towards the coral.

His Appaloosa stood ready and alert, listening for any sign of approach. Ben found the corral in the increasing darkness, and blew a short, low whistle. The beaten mustang was long gone, and the stallion tossed its head at Ben's nearness. Ben reached for the rope halter around its neck and made the old soothing noises as he kicked out the corral bars. He held the stallion's head down close, and led it away back to the bleak deserted outskirts of the town.

Out beyond the tents and flophouses, he found a shack big enough to shelter them. It was well removed and hidden from the main street and buildings of the town. Ben had to get to the livery stable, then find a few provisions. He made sure the stallion was secure, and for reassurance draped the remnants of his deerskin coat around its neck. As he set out for the livery stable, the first drops of water spattered through the rotted eaves of the shack.

The smithy was sitting in a room annexed to the stable. There was lamplight, and Ben could see the remains of a beating across the side of the man's face. He tapped the open door with his foot and spoke softly. 'Looks like you broke off your engagement with them soldier friends.'

The smithy looked up, startled. He dropped a broadsheet and gripped the sides of his chair. 'Who the . . . ? Jeezus, it's you. You come back.'

Ben stepped in close from the stable. 'They certainly didn't waste their time in comin' for me. Findin' me was *real* clever, an' they took my horse.'

The smithy stared past Ben, out into the heavy, increasing rain. 'That would be McKay, the scout. It was Pelt's long game, enticin' you in. It's always goin' to be on *his* ground, not yours. But they didn't expect you back, no one did.' He looked unbelieving at Ben. 'You've risked your life to get the stallion?'

Ben crouched, facing the beaten blacksmith. 'Yeah, amongst other things. And now you're riskin' yours. You go find 'em; tell 'em I'm here waitin'.'

The smithy climbed slowly from his chair. 'They'll come tomorrow, all off 'em. The captain will want to know your name.'

Ben turned away and walked from the stable 'They'll all go to Hell wonderin' that. An' like most people in this town, you're forgettin' he ain't a captain no more.'

When he returned to the shack he found some horse mash, half a bottle of whiskey, a wedge of cheese and a pail of clean water. 'That's a real neat trick,' he muttered. Now he wouldn't have to search for any fodder, because someone knew he was there and was trying to help. He lifted his boot against some straw on the floor and saw that his Sharps rifle had gone. Ben had an odd feeling of who'd been there, who'd followed him in the darkness. His mind flicked to the image he'd seen earlier, way off along the stream.

The rain had advanced across the town, and it beat on the thin roofing. The storm's power was growing, and under its intensity Ben curled into a corner with the cheese. He had a mouthful of whiskey and cleaned his face and hands with the rest. He settled for a few hours of thought, and preparation of his mind. Not a secure lodge, but good enough for one final night, and he knew there was an ally somewhere near.

21

It was nearly mid-morning, and there was no more thunder, just seething rain. A solid deluge, that in twelve hours had flooded Lizard Wells from its north and south perimeters to the banks of the Piney; an arid township changed to fifty acres of swollen waterflats. Cans and bottles eddied their way into the street, floating for moments before capsizing where the torrent was deepest. Barrel staves, fence rails, a tent, drowned rats, drifted and turned aimlessly through the channels of sidewalk and alleyway. There were no sounds other than the clamour of falling water and the incessant hiss on the red-brown slurry of manure and kindling.

Where rain funnelled down from the shakes, Ben had waited patiently between the string of huggered buildings. He knew his only chance was to take the soldiers separately, and on his own terms. Their arrival and deployment presented a chance for slaughter, and he could probably do it, but that was their way, not his.

Four men checked their mounts, and sat unmoved alongside Pelt. Ben could see that the guerrilla captain was considering a way to use them. He wasn't going to be rushed; he would take advantage of the weather and the territory. He twisted in the saddle and nodded out his line-up. Water flashed and spouted from the drooping brim of his hat, and he tugged nervously at his sodden gauntlets. As one man they dismounted, slapping their horses to send them galloping and sloshing back towards the empty corral at the end of town. Dragging their hats down low, they moved cautiously into the street. Their boot-tops glistened black below oiled slickers, and their hands and arms clutched a variety of Colts and carbines.

Ben edged himself forward, hardly

one pace, through a sliding sheet of water. It streamed from his head and filled his ears, and the crash of rain turned blunt and muffled. He flicked his head sharply from side to side and hefted the Navy Colt, wrapping its cinch tight around his wrist. He didn't intend to telegraph an invitation to any of these men. It was one against five, and he had to start shooting. He brought up the gun and stood sideways on, his body partially hidden by a broken swinging door.

He fired two shots, low into the cluster of soldiers, knowing that at least one would go down. A tall, grey-bearded trooper dropped his rifle, lurched one pace backward, then one forward. He clutched his groin and spat towards Ben, trying to penetrate the rain. Then he turned his head away, and pitched sideways into the water.

A barrage of lead crashed around the boardwalk, splintering the loose panels of the door and uprights of a low veranda. Ben slithered sideways along the alley, and backed into a doorway at the rear of a dry-goods store. He shoved his Colt at an old woman who sat quietly clutching a small bundle of muddy fur. She sniggered at him, and Ben told her to shut up. He listened for the frenzied slash of feet through water, but although he heard a sharp command from Pelt, there was only the continuing sound of rain, and an irked yelp from the mongrel. He paused in the narrow yard at the back of the store, and blew water from the chambers of his Colt. He knew they wouldn't follow him into the alleyways. Captain Pelt favoured the open, and head-on against the weaponless. They weren't sure where he was, and none of them wanted to be next.

Alert to any marginal sound or movement, he worked his way to within fifty feet of the livery stable. Visibility was just that far, and he could make out the grain-gate in the end of the upper storey. Above the stalls was a risky position with no way out, but he could look down on the street. He heard a yell from close by, and felt a thump above his elbow, then pain, as the scorch bruised into his upper arm. He sucked in a deep breath and grazed the wound with the barrel of his Colt. The pain wouldn't get any worse than that.

Likenesses of medicine men and Cheyenne dancers, self-mutilated and painted with white clay, flashed through Ben's mind.

'*O, Sun, I do this for you!*'

The soldiers were going to press and harry. They'd lost him once, but now having marked him, they were comparatively safe, and more sure of themselves.

Another bullet clanged and whined off the iron hitching rail that ran into the open doors of the stables ahead of him. As he ran across the open ground, he heard Pelt shout a warning. He glanced over his shoulder and saw two men burst out from either side of a building across the narrow street. It was Ketchum, and Bolton McKay, the army scout.

Pelt yelled again at McKay. The scout was running and pointing towards the blacksmith's yard as a bullet took him in the back of the neck. He stopped, straightened up, then staggered back with short staccato steps. He buckled sideways, grappling at the cape of Ketchum, and collapsed against the boardwalk steps, his throat a spiralling wash of pink and red. Ketchum shoved himself free of the scout, and brought his rifle to bear on Ben's running figure. Ahead of him Ben saw a window frame shatter as he skewed towards the stable.

Breath was rasping in his throat, and more bullets were tearing into the buildings ahead of him. He vaulted the blacksmith's fence, then veered into the livery stable. He jumped onto the top of an empty crate and rolled himself awkwardly up into the low rafters of the hay loft. The straw was decaying, and the grain bags were swollen and musted with long storage. Ben let his Colt hang on its cinch, and grabbed at the tie-rope of one of the sacks. He levered himself into a sitting position, and shouldered one of the heavy bags into a corner of the grain-gate.

Down below, the rib mule stomped nervously in its stall, and Ben knew that it was only a matter of seconds before Pelt or Ketchum wondered about the noise, and the bullet that killed McKay. He fell forward onto his right shoulder and gathered his Colt into his waist. He looked down, but saw only the rats scuttling around the animal pelts and humps of dried meat. Two of them were gnawing at the pad of a bear cub that lay shrunk and lifeless in a wooden crate. He pointed the long barrel of his Colt down at the rats. He cocked the hammer and took deliberate aim on a fat scuttling shape. Another bullet, but what the hell, Pelt or Ketchum would probably kill him anyway.

Ben turned away as the rat exploded beneath him. Fur scraps, and a crimson bloom burst into the mud, and the crash bellowed around the stable. He pushed himself up again and peered into the rain that still drilled down a few inches from his face. He made out the blurry figure of the second trooper near the front of the hotel. He carried two army revolvers and was staring about him nervously, trying to make a fix on the gunshot. Ben watched him thoughtfully as he sidled across the street, signalling one of his guns at Pelt, who crouched motionless beside an overflowed butt.

Two men dead, three more to go, Ben thought. He could see two of them now, but where was Ketchum?

In the middle of the street, the trooper stepped into the broken spokes of a rig wheel. He cursed and, as he jerked at his foot, he briefly lost his balance. It was the chance that Ben needed.

It was a two-handed, single shot, and it took the trooper low in the chest. His foot was still wedged, and he fell flat and stretched across the half-submerged wheel. Pelt threw himself sideways, out of sight and almost beneath Ben. He was now close against the trough that fronted the pen of the blacksmith's yard.

Now there were two, but they pinpointed him. He was caught in his own trap — had sought the disadvantage. Unless he dropped into the stalls, there was no escape, other than a twenty-foot jump from the grain-gate into Pelt's firing line.

He fired at a running shadow at the edge of his vision, saw the man stumble, pick himself up again and hobble under cover. It was Lieutenant Ketchum, and a mistake to have missed. A bullet slashed into the woodwork near his hand, and he pulled back sharply. *Let them come*, shouted a furious voice at the back of his mind. And then much quieter and less hopeful, *come into the open*. But they wouldn't do that. They preferred their victims trapped, like those around Horse Creek Lakes.

He thumbed the chamber of his Colt.

One bullet left, and he lay waiting for them to make their move.

A hail of bullets was the response from Ketchum and Pelt, and Ben slid back into the piled up straw. Sweat ran into his eyes, and he rubbed it away with the crook of his arm. He clambered quickly from the loft, wincing from his wound and the withering fire that poured up through the grain-gate. Hanks of roofing were being torn away, and rain immediately shafted in above him. The mule was lashing out at the rear of his stall and his pale eyes bulged with fright. Manure beneath its feet was steaming fresh, and tufted lumps splattered up and touched Ben's hands and face.

Then he had the feeling of not being alone. Another sensation fused the heavy atmosphere and, cautiously raising his gun hand, he half-turned to encounter it. For the first time he was aware of the squeals from the rats, and then another sound. He felt pressure in his head, then the bestial noises and reek of the livery stable intensified, before exploding in a chaos of black. There was a stab of awareness, time for another feeling of not being alone, as he was lowered gently across a pile of rope and damp sacking.

★ ★ ★

In her small nest of rooms above the saloon, Erma Flagg shouted at Derby Crewes, the town's sheriff. 'It's your chance, Derby. Go an' help 'em. As long as that wild trash runs you an' the town, we'll never have anythin'. Can't you see, it's comin' to an end? It's happenin' out there, right now, and you're lettin' a boy do what you should be doin'.' Erma's words hammered against the sheriff. 'If anythin' happens to Moses today, I swear I'll shoot you dead myself.'

Crewes was staring blank-eyed down into the street. The water was shafting into the room from the half-open window, and he hardly bothered to make himself heard above the storm. He didn't turn to face Erma, he was listening to the muffled sound of gunfire. Now and again he saw pallid figures sloshing in and out of the alleys below. 'I'm sorry. It's too late now, Erma. I'm not up to it anymore.'

They both knew he was choking back the fear of being caught in the crossfire between Captain Pelt and his renegades and Ben Brooke — maybe Moses.

Erma walked towards the sheriff and took a shot-gun from his slackening grasp. 'You were never up to it, Derby. My ol' ma's got a stiffer backbone than you, an' she's been under a clod for ten years. Whatever happens here, I won't be back again, unless it's to come lookin' for you.'

In frustration and disgust, Erma grabbed the ancient forage cap from her head and threw it against Crewes' back. She glanced at the rawness of her home, saw herself in the hanging mirror. She grimaced at the murky reflection, then moved onto the staircase. It led to the deluge below, and she was instantly soaked to her skin. There was an incredible run of water around her face, and she tipped down the barrel of the shotgun. The once mud-packed street had become a foaming lake, and she stepped onto the adjoining boardwalk. Even across the street she couldn't see the livery stable or the hotel. The buildings were no more than a wavering deception.

There was no more gunfire, and Erma tried to recall where the last heard shots had come from. She stepped back under the lean of the staircase to reckon the whereabouts of Moses.

22

Moses had a short but concerned look at Ben, then moved quickly to the rear stalls. He showed the palm of his hand to quieten the mule, and watched the saw-flies return to their rich pickings. Out in front, Pelt and Ketchum were alive, but he'd seen one of them wounded.

The odds were good, and he stepped quickly away from the stable and across the blacksmith's yard. Pelt was moving almost directly under the grain-gate in the stable, and unseen by Moses. The shooting had stopped, and the Cheyenne half-breed cut through into the street less than thirty yards down from the livery stable. Nothing moved — an empty town under a shimmering curtain of rain.

His young muscles steadied. His eyes tunnelled straight ahead, but relaxed for the slightest movement to show. He walked calmly into the full body of rain, and it hammered into his body. He wanted it, the painful bite and freshness of the conflict, and he coolly levered another round into the Sharps rifle.

There was a change to a shape off the street, and he swung the big gun to cover. His reflection fluttered thin and watery from the window of the hotel — a timely sharpener to the situation. He sidled over to the claps of the few remaining cabins that reached out from the stable. He half expected some sort of sign, but nothing moved, and he stepped back into the alleyway and edged back to where he'd started from.

He reached the rear door and glanced swiftly into the gloom. The flood water had spread thin manure across the stable, and the rats were weaving through the garbage. He swiped his hand at the humidity and thick buzz of the flies. There was no response from Ketchum or Pelt, just Ben, numbed and very still beneath the hay loft.

Had Captain Gideon Pelt decided to stand-off his last campaign, with his men either dead or wounded? Perhaps he had decided to pull out while there was still time — preferable to a bullet from Ben Brooke. Moses doubted it and stepped away.

Out in the street, branched on the rig-wheel, was a dead trooper. A small garter snake swam into the oilskin that bloated around his neck in the swirling water. Twenty minutes previously from Erma's room above the saloon, Moses had watched another man drag himself agonizingly under the slats of a broken timber wagon. Ben Brooke had brought them both down with belly shots.

Just beyond the saloon, Moses saw the body of McKay; the one they'd called The Dead Meat. He was lying where he'd shot him with Ben's Springfield from the same room. He was sprawled against low steps, arms outflung and legs crumpled beneath his oilskin. Moses knew then that Pelt and Ketchum — if they were still in Lizard

Wells — were alone.

Slowly he pushed along the street, an unbroken spread of noise falling into him from every side. Was Pelt hidden in a street-shack, or lee of an alleyway, ready to shoot him without warning? Maybe he'd decided to ride out into the blur and obscurity of the Breaks. Moses doubted that as well.

He moved forward carefully, but apart from gunfire, rain chopped up all sound, and he didn't hear the light splash as someone trod the flanking boards of the hotel. He just caught a timber creak, as the boom and wild reverberation of a shotgun exploded close behind him. His body contracted, waiting for the searing red punch in the middle of his back. It didn't happen, but he saw Pelt looming from a passageway directly across the street, his slicker draped neatly around the shiny barrel of an Army Colt. Moses knew immediately that something must have happened to Ketchum, and he flung himself forward, his body arched to avoid the depth of water. He stretched out his right arm in line with the stock of the carbine, his forefinger coiled around the trigger.

Pelt reacted instantly and fired. It ploughed down into the muddied water and stung Moses' eyes as he squeezed the trigger. In a second, he twisted to his side, and with one hand levered another shell into the carbine and fired again, blindly. Pelt stopped in mid-stride, as the first bullet hit. Then he snapped forward, as the second took him at waist level, destroying his gun and half an arm at the same time. There was an expression of astonishment on his face as he stared down at wrist bones that were jellied to his gun and shredded slicker. He struck a hitching rail, and it collapsed. With one hand he clutched at the string of his sodden hat, then he closed his eyes and fell. He turned over as slow as a fat timbered log, and rain and mud slipped from the carve of his face. He mouthed something across at Moses, but he didn't open his eyes. Only his boots moved, spurs digging the water in frustration and defeat.

Moses eased himself onto his knees, and scraped water down from his hair across his face. He blinked clearness back into his eyes, and jammed the butt of the Springfield into the ground. He pressed his forehead against the barrel, and felt the curious warmth.

Ketchum's body was wrapped and shrouded beneath his slicker. His hat was trapped floating, and covered the top part of his face. His eyes would be staring upward, unseeing, and his mouth was open, filling with bright clean water. A darker ribbon welled from his chest, spreading slowly, almost touching Moses.

On the boards, one arm around an upright, Erma was leaning forward, her face drained like chalk. Cold and unemotional she stared across the body, her lips trembling, trying to force a sound. She took a faltering step towards Moses, and he put his arm up. It was an instinctive and natural, *hey come on, ma*, backlash, and he tugged at the trouser material above her muddy boots. The shotgun dropped from her fingers, and it clattered off the wood before splashing under the water. The rain continued to thrash around them, but he knew the bright salty rills down Erma's face were free-flowing for him.

★   ★   ★

Five army horses cantered down the narrow street. They were bunched tight, agitated and wary. Water glimmered on their empty saddles, and their dark coats steamed. They tossed their heavy necks, and their reins snapped patterns in the rain. They would run to the corral then back again, until eventually somebody stopped them.

★   ★   ★

It was the following morning and the storm had moved on. First light threw its pale colours across the muddied Piney, and Moses stood motionless in the racing water. It was the same stance that Ben had seen thirty-six hours earlier, and it triggered his feelings and wits. The son who for ten years he'd never known, who'd survived the massacre at Horse Creek Lakes. Erma had got it right. When Ben had shot the first two men outside of the hotel, she'd worked it out, made a card player's guess at the chances.

Moses turned towards Ben and Erma who were sitting together on the bank. He asked about his Indian name, giving Ben some more moments of thoughtful anguish.

'It's a long time past, an' Moses is a good name . . . a very good name,' Ben said in due course. 'Let's both let it go.'

Moses still looked at his father. 'Those men you killed . . . the one I shot?' He had trouble finding the words, making the personal connection. 'They did the killing at the Lakes?'

'Yeah. What I did, was all I ever set

out to do, Moses. It all seems such a long time ago.'

The boy wanted to know. He was still worried and needed the explanation. 'And that soldier . . . the second one in the street . . . the one who said he wasn't army. Was he there?'

'Yeah, he was there. He was a liar too . . . got his soul badly damaged by it.'

From watching Ben, Erma turned to Moses. 'We all had a hand in that, an' it's right that we did. In a way it's what families are for.' She thought she heard Ben gulp, but she didn't look at him. 'But it holds nothin', an' the past's been laid to rest. None of us is ever goin' to forget, but the memories will fade . . . eventually.' Then she did glance at Ben. 'For all of us.' Moses waded from the water and crouched on the opposite bank.

Ben looked over his shoulder at the storm-ravaged town. 'Ain't a lot to go back to, Erma.'

'So it ain't a lot to leave,' she said tellingly.

23

The snow was knee deep and, when the door swung open, a cloud of fresh, drifting flakes billowed into the warmth of the cabin.

Erma looked up, and a snug, comfortable smile softened the years. Moses was lying in a hammock, tying fish hooks to line. He twisted round as the door thudded shut.

'Look, ain't that my pa?' he shouted jokily.

Ben stomped into the big room and looked around him, renewed the comforting sights and smells.

Erma got up, smoothed down the front of her dress and took a bowl from the stove. She knew that Ben had been back to Lizard Wells. 'What was it like?' She looked at Moses as she spoke, and her eyes twinkled.

It had been almost a year since the